FAHRENHEIT
1600

JERRY WEBER

D1004701

DocUmeant *Publishing*
244 5th Avenue
Suite G-200
NY. NY 10001
646-233-4366
www.DocUmeantPublishing.com

Fahrenheit 1600
bk 1: Victor Kozol Series

Published by
DocUmeant Publishing
244 5th Avenue, Suite G-200
NY, NY 10001

Phone: 6462334366
http://www.DocUmeantPublishing.com

Disclaimer: This is a work of fiction. Names, characters, businesses, places, events and incidents are either the products of the author's imagination or used in a fictitious manner. Any resemblance to real persons, living or dead is purely coincidental with the exception of a few famous individuals and locations mentioned briefly. Celebrities or locations mentioned in this work do not represent endorsements by them, their heirs, or any business mentioned in this work of fiction.

Library of Congress Control Number: 2016944191

ISBN13: 978-1-937801-69-4
ISBN10: 1-937801-69-1

Dedication

To my wife, Cynthia. Thank you for not allowing *Fahrenheit 1600* to be relegated to the dust bin.

To Linda and Joe
To all the
good years.

Jerry

Contents

Acknowledgments

THE IDEA FOR this novel is mine, but it never would have gotten to you without the help of many other people. First, my loving wife of forty-six years told me, after I let the project drop for three years, to revive it. She saw it as a good tale that should be published. Thank you Cynthia.

Secondly, my two daughters have each given me help and input into the finished product. Natalie helped me shape it and provided the 80s culture and music input along with streamlining clumsy syntax and added ideas and a character like Sophie. She has a mind more fertile than mine and has spent much time helping from Berlin, Germany where she and her family reside.

Annette, my older daughter from Baltimore, helped me navigate the inscrutable menus of a computer word processor. She tried her best to bring me into the twenty first century with digital formats. All of you have cheered me on and forced me to see this thing through. I can't say thank you enough.

Patti Knoles, how can I begin to thank you for your patience and talent in bringing my book to life with your extraordinary cover design? You are true jewel. I'll be back with book two.

To Philip and Ginger Marks editor and publisher; I had no experience in this field and you two have made it easy and possible for me to complete this work. Thank you.

Prologue

WILKES-BARRE, PA. CIRCA 1984 is a small city situated on the banks of the Susquehanna River in the northeast Pennsylvania anthracite coal region. Three blocks south of the business district, South Franklin Street is a peaceful street in a residential neighborhood. The large Victorian homes that line this bucolic street speak of a bygone era when coal barons, professionals, and business people inhabited the neighborhood.

Depending on whom you asked, the city's name was pronounced as either "bear" or "berry"—even by the locals. In any event, Wilkes University had been slowly buying up the properties in a several square block area with plans to expand since the 1940s.

Just south of the University's main campus, the two hundred block of South Franklin Street has had several of its larger buildings converted into college dormitories. Many of the remaining old mansions have long since been turned into apartment buildings. This urban campus became an island of prosperity in a post industrial town that has, like most American cities, seen significant change.

Sophie Lunitis is the owner of one of these Franklin Street buildings, a quadplex brick structure built around 1900. Sophie and her husband Joseph purchased the building thirty years before as a place to live and provide an income. They had the old mansion divided into four apartments; theirs was on the first floor and there were three for rent.

After retiring and living together for twenty years, Joseph died from a heart attack. This left Sophie to carry on alone—they had no children. For the first two decades, many from the Lithuanian community, along with the ethnic Poles and Italians and others who once worked the coal mines and later retired, lived in Sophie's building. But in the last ten years, many of her tenants either died or moved on.

The only real opportunities to rent for a good price came from Wilkes University students. Sophie didn't like most of the students. She came from another generation; one might even say another world. Hers was an era using last names and shaking hands and of ladies who wore hats and gloves.

Her ethnic background also meant that Sophie was, well, one might say she was the first environmentalist. Sophie treated just about everything, including tap water, like a scarce resource that could run out at any moment if not carefully rationed. Perhaps it was some ancestral memory from Eastern Europe, where the difference between making it through the winter and starving to death was this ability to see the value in every scrap of cloth and crumb of bread.

As a consequence, Sophie had something of a hoarding tendency. There were those old flannel shirts she meant to cut up into rags and Danish butter cookie tins she was going to sort her button collection into, but she did have the lowest electricity bill on the block—perhaps even the state.

The way her new tenants, a generation of spoiled kids who thought "money grew on trees" (a favorite expression of Sophie's), wasted resources drove Sophie into apoplectic fits. She was not above pounding furiously on the door to the apartment above her if she heard a shower running for too long. This often led some of the young women to shriek that she had no right to invade their privacy. Undaunted, Sophie would inevitably retort that they had "No right to waste good water someone else might need."

"I'm pretty sure there's enough to go around," one tenant had responded her voice dripping with sarcasm as she looked at the little old woman with something like pity.

"Is that so? Well, I'm not so sure you're the best person to judge. What is it you study, basket weaving?"

"Sociology" the young woman replied through gritted teeth.

"Well, you're not a civil engineer or geologist, that's for sure, and if you do manage to use up all the water around here, you'll have a hard time dyeing your hair that trashy color or washing all that makeup off your face, so you might want to go easy on things." Indeed, the young woman had blue eyeliner streaming from one eye and her hair was an unnatural yellow.

Sophie had turned and marched down the stairs to her apartment after this altercation, feeling vindicated and happy for the opportunity to educate the next generation in the ways of this world.

The young woman, on the other hand, had called half a dozen friends to recount her unprovoked abuse at the hands of her landlady (with several dramatic embellishments), lost hours of sleep over "the nerve of that woman," contemplated moving out, realized it was too much effort, and then, finally, stayed. She also, although it was something she never consciously admitted to herself, stopped taking such long showers and switched to a blond hair dye with more ash tones.

Sophie wasn't one to lose arguments once she started them and she started them often.

True to her highly conservative nature, Sophie never took out the anthracite coal boiler in her basement. This meant that every day she had to load fresh coal into her stoker hopper. This was a semi-automatic gravity-fed device that saved shoveling into the fire several times a day. However, every other day her coal furnace created heaps of ashes from the burnt coal which had to be carried out in pails. At seventy and alone, Sophie, as sharp and agile physically as she was mentally, could still do this job. Knowing that she was paying less for heat than many of her neighbors was all the motivation she needed. She also secretly enjoyed the idea that she produced her own ashes for covered her slippery driveway during winter while her neighbors—the spendthrift fools—would buy bags of salt at the local store.

The only downside to this was that she would inevitably come home on a wintry day to see a window wide open with her precious heat escaping. Nothing made Sophie angrier.

"Victor!" she bellowed up the stairs towards Victor Kozol's apartment, "I said I provide heat for you not the entire city!"

"Okay, Sophie, I'll take care of it." Still, the guilty party, a young man by the name of Victor Kozol, was not in any hurry to close the window. After all, even that old witch Sophie might know what marijuana smells like.

Victor was a first-year pre-med student from Duryea, a town about eight miles away and was upstairs indulging in a well-deserved rest after carrying up the last of the beer, wine, and other supplies for his latest party. It was scheduled for tonight, so he needed to marshal his strength. Victor inhaled deeply and wondered just how problematic his landlady was going to be.

Sophie was thinking, "Things were different in the 'good old days'. Old Doc Francis, the founding president of Wilkes didn't allow alcohol to be served anywhere on campus, and that included faculty events. Francis was known to threaten local neighborhood bar owners not to serve his under 21 students unless they wanted to hear from the Pennsylvania Liquor Control Board. And, of course, alcohol was not allowed in college dormitories. Yes, things were a lot quieter and much better back then," Sophie thought.

In the early hours of Saturday morning Sophie found herself in her kitchen fuming, she has once again banged on the hot water pipes going up to Victor's apartment which is directly above hers.

"Silence," she yelled, "it's after midnight!"

"When we were these students' age, we had to get to sleep so we could get to work the next day," Sophie thought, angrily. Her not-so fond remembrances of her summer working at a button factory in Scranton were rudely interrupted by a blood-curdling scream. Sophie looked out her kitchen window just in time to catch a fleeting glimpse of a young coed in a chair fall into the evergreen bush behind her back porch. It was 1:00 a.m. and soon sirens are blaring.

Within minutes an ambulance backed into the driveway beside her home to the scene of the accident. Sophie couldn't believe it; the young girl was actually limping away towards the ambulance with assistance from the paramedics.

"Vai tu zmogau" she hollers in Lithuanian, "How's she not dead? This is the last straw," thought Sophie. "Victor must go."

Directly above Sophie, Victor is sitting in his trashed living room, wondering how such a fun-filled and lucrative evening could go so wrong. This Friday, Vic had done his usual thing. He sold tickets to twenty students he knew from campus for $10.00 each. He then schlepped the beer, wine, and other supplies up the steps all afternoon to prepare for the event. With $200.00 income, Vic had doubled his money. He mused to himself, this is how you enjoy college life and make spending money on the side. Life was good. Good until Jake dared Allison to balance on a chair out on the fire escape landing railing. It still could have ended cool, but Charley needed another beer and bumped the chair leg trying to squeeze by; thus propelling Allison fifteen feet down into the bushes. Why did ten people have to want to smoke outside on the fire escape at the same time? Do these college students have no brains?

Two days later, Victor was sitting in front of Dr. Scharter, the Dean of Men at Wilkes. This time the party hit the front page of the "Times Leader"—the local newspaper. While the paper stated that Allison was treated and released from the hospital, Victor was not going to have an easy time of it. Dr. Scharter went through the usual bromides about the college and its image and relationship with the community, personal responsibility, and whatever else is usually said at these meetings. Victor was given social probation for the rest of the year and warned that the next time there would be no need for a meeting. What Scharter didn't know at the time, since it was only mid-term, was that Victor was missing half of his classes and flunking or getting D's in most of his subjects. None of this boded well for Vic's continuation at Wilkes.

The Kozols

THE TOWN OF Duryea lies midway between Scranton and Wilkes-Barre, the two largest cities in northeastern Pennsylvania, themselves more like large towns. Claiming a population of 140,000 in the 1930s, Scranton is now just a fraction of its former size. Only about 80,000 remain by the late 1980s and the demographic is aging. Wilkes-Barre experienced a similar decline, sinking from 70,000 to 40,000 during the same period. With six thousand residents, Duryea, like so many other small towns that benefited from the area's coal mines, is also a smaller place than it was fifty years ago.

Northeastern Pennsylvania once supplied the entire East Coast with anthracite, the hard coal preferred for heating homes, hotels, and factories. They all benefited from an energy source that was cheap and plentiful. But after World War II, the government ended its rationing of oil and gas. These two competing fossil fuels from places far away like Oklahoma and Texas were soon flooding eastward to power the booming American economy. By the 1950s, most residences and businesses had abandoned coal and switched to oil burners or gas furnaces. The reason was simple. Heat from furnaces powered by these fuels could be more easily regulated and there was no solid by-product (coal cinders) to dispose of. What was left after combustion went into the air and it would be decades before anyone cared much about that.

America in the late 1980s was still a time of profligate energy consumption. Cars were big and woefully inefficient, gas and oil was a negligible extra expense, but few people in the "Coal Regions" drove their pickup trucks to a mine. Instead, they transitioned to whatever service jobs as could be found with the government, the large local hospitals, and some industrial plants sprinkled throughout the area—or they simply left.

The Kozol family was fortunate not to have to change occupations with the times. Victor's father ran a family-owned funeral business that was established over fifty years ago by his father, and death was one of few constants in America's shifting cultural and economic landscape. People died and it still cost a good bit of money to respectfully transition bodies to ash or earth. The area's aging population was good for business, to be sure, but this boon was offset by a declining overall population base.

Victor, his parents, and a sister who was three years older lived in an apartment above the funeral home in the center of Duryea. Victor's father, Albert, never had more than the one year of post high school education required to receive a funeral director's license in the state of Pennsylvania. He always hoped his two children would get four year degrees and, in Victor's case, maybe become a doctor. Victor's sister, Anne, had always been very self-driven and decided to attend Wilkes University. She majored in elementary education and became a teacher. Anne also met another young teacher while earning her educational credits and got married. Albert had nephews living down state who were both doctors. He, of course, would like nothing better than to match his brothers with a doctor of his own in the family.

Not one to leave things to chance, Albert took Victor aside during his junior year at Duryea High School and told him about the great future he could have in medicine.

"I believe that every generation should do a little better than the one before it," said Albert as he began his rehearsed "American Dream" speech. "My grandfather, after emigrating from Poland, worked in the mines and then died at the age of fifty with miner's asthma (aka black lung disease). My father, not wanting to suffer the same fate, got involved in the funeral business by helping an old undertaker. Later he started his own business; and I was proud to run it when I left school, but the area isn't what it was. You don't have to be stuck here, Victor. Getting a medical or legal degree is the next step up the ladder. If you're a doctor or a lawyer, you can move anywhere you like. Look at your sister Anne. She has tenure and a guaranteed income from teaching. Of course, due to the nature of our business and the things you've been exposed to, I imagine you'd have a leg up in medicine, and we'd be willing to help with the tuition fees."

Victor's mind immediately filled with images of himself pulling into a large hospital in a new Mercedes Roadster. His parking spot would have a plaque, "Reserved for Dr. Kozol."

"Is this something you're interested in?" Albert asked, interrupting Victor's reverie.

"I think so, yes." Victor said.

Albert smiled. The problem was that Victor would say anything to his father to get more allowance or use of the family car. He was only average in school because he didn't study, but he was smart enough to not flunk or get D's in his courses. He was never motivated to excel, but he was able to score pretty high on his SATs, so college was definitely going to be available to him. Victor's real talents were more social. He was one of the more popular kids in high school. He always had something to do; the phone was usually for him.

In his senior year, Vic was no National Merit Scholar, but his SATs allowed him, along with his father's ability to pay the tuition, to get accepted by two local colleges. With his father's guidance and cajoling, Vic chose Wilkes University in Wilkes-Barre and selected pre-med as his major. On a bright and cheerful September day, the family dropped Vic off at his new apartment on South Franklin Street.

"I hope you have time to come and visit us some weekends with all your studying," a somewhat delusional Albert said as he shook his son's hand goodbye.

"Oh, I'll try, Dad," promised Victor, his eyes looking over his father's shoulder observing a freshman coed in cut-off jeans who looked like she could use some help moving a box.

As his parents' station wagon pulled out of view, his mother waving from the passenger seat, a feeling of euphoria overcame Victor. For the first time in his life he was completely free. He was also no longer in Duryea. While Wilkes-Barre was not exactly a big city, he didn't know every single girl here since grade school. The possibilities were endless.

Wilkes University wasn't a big school and it wasn't Ivy League, but what it lacked in prestige it made up for in charm and friendliness. It was the gateway to the professions for many local first generation college students. Most of the resident students lived in dormitories converted from the former homes of the industrial magnates who built the town on the Susquehanna River during the last century. But Victor was even luckier. He convinced his parents to let him live in an off campus apartment right away; on the grounds that it would cost the same and would give him more privacy to study. An advertisement on a campus message board in front of the library was full of offers from students looking for roommates. There was no housing shortage in this slowly contracting former coal town.

Victor had contacted Andy Moyer, whom he met once over the summer. Andy was a computer science major and conformed to type: Lanky dark hair cut in a mullet, or perhaps simply allowed to grow that way, low-effort clothing choices consisting usually of sweat pants, free T-shirts, and glasses. He was an otherwise attractive young man, but socially awkward and eager to please the confident young Victor. He also really needed a roommate to help pay the rent after his former roommate graduated.

For his part, Victor immediately liked the college senior's indifferent approach to house cleaning. The apartment was the standard undergraduate man cave of pizza boxes, dirty socks, and Led Zeppelin posters, but Victor knew it would be perfect for his designs and just hoped that Andy didn't get in the way. The key would be to get into his new roommates good graces right from the start. To this end, Victor set up his stereo system in the living room where Andy could also use it instead of in his room and set about rolling a joint after stowing away his other possessions. The stereo blasted "Kashmir."

"Oh man, you know, I'm such a big Zeppelin fan." Andy said, cracking open a cola and wiping a bit of sweat from his brow after having helped move exactly two of Victor's boxes upstairs.

Victor feigned surprise, took a largish toke on the joint, stretched luxuriantly and asked, "So, what's the plan this weekend?"

"I hadn't planned much. Maybe have some guys over to watch the game tomorrow."

"So what, aren't there any big parties the first weekend?" Victor's visions of college life were largely informed by repeat viewings of *Animal House*. "What about the fraternities and sororities?"

"Wilkes doesn't have any. The founder, Dr. Francis, felt they promote 'elitism' and banned them. It's one of those things about this place you'll get used to." Andy shrugged.

"So what's the policy on throwing a party of our own?" What's the landlady like?

A jolt of dread went through Andy at the thought of Sophie, the building's owner and formidable custodian, but he didn't want to admit to fearing an elderly woman before his younger, but clearly hipper companion.

"Oh, she's pretty cool. I haven't had any problems with her."

This was true, but largely because Andy did little else but write computer programs and play Dungeons and Dragons with some other CS majors at the kitchen table. Andy always had the feeling, though, from the cold stares Sophie gave him when he met her on the stairs that she wasn't someone he'd want to cross.

Victor's mind strategized like a chess player when it came to his own pleasures. He had already come to the conclusion that Andy's friend base was not going to make for a good party, nor would his dorky roommate likely know where any of the good parties would be held. He himself didn't know anyone, but that was no barrier. Weren't parties all about getting to know people?

"Why don't we throw a party?"

"What? When?" Andy stammered.

"Tomorrow. I'll make some fliers. We can charge ten bucks a head or do you think that's too much."

"I don't know. . ."

"Okay, then five. You're 21, right?"

"Well, yah, but."

"Perfect. I've got a bit of cash to stock the place in the beginning. Once we get a crowd, you can always go for a beer run. It we get cheap stuff like Stegmaier or Old Milwaukee, we should even be able to turn a profit on this."

"I guess . . ."

"Great! Well, I guess we should start making the flyers."

In a flight of creativity, Victor created Wilkes University's first ever' Freshman Fete', although the crowd was not limited to freshman nor even to college students. Anyone with a fiver got in and Victor became a minor celebrity on campus.

As Andy had feared, however, this course of events was neither unnoticed nor approved of by Sophie who lived on the first floor. The pair were awakened most Sunday mornings by an ill-tempered yet vigorous old woman decked out in her Church-going clothes complete with hat and handbag. The visit was meant to be both a punishment for the severely hungover young men and a shaming rebuke for their behavior, although the latter aim was lost on Andy and Victor. For them, Sunday morning was little more than a void they filled with dreamless sleep.

Sophie would have loved nothing better to throw them both out, but things weren't what they used to be in Wilke-Barre. Between the junkie on the 2nd floor and the lady who kept strange hours across the hall from her, the other clientele in her building were nothing to be proud of.

College students were at least somewhat respectable. It was also usually possible to get their parents to pay for larger repairs from the damage they caused, and no matter how bad they were they always left after a few years. By the look of this new kid, Sophie was guessing he wouldn't be around for very long. And, as in most things, her utterly unsentimental nature was spot on. Victor's social life was on a collision course with his, or rather his father's, dream of him becoming doctor.

College Life

BY JANUARY, THE verdant green hills surrounding Wilkes-Barre turned brown as the temperatures hovered in the twenties. Brisk biting wind swept down along the Susquehanna River penetrating even the heaviest coats. Life had moved inside, but this was a boon for Victor: His shindigs had become so well-known around campus that they are by invitation only, a triumph for Victor's social life and finances. Each party usually cleared about $100, after beverages were factored in. During this time, Victor's chief source of anxiety had been keeping Sophie at bay and not getting evicted. And yet Victor's party enterprise iron-ically brought him closer to Sophie's own anxieties as he had to contend with his own irresponsible "temporary tenants." A recent party guest managed to smash the toilet so badly, Victor had to fork over $300.00 for a replacement.

Then there was the little matter of the summons from the Wilkes-Barre police for excessive noise and disturbing the peace; and if Sophie thought Victor was hard to pin-down for his many transgressions, the pseudo-anonymous party set that flowed in and out of Vic's apartment was impossible to bring to account. Yet the party money continued and outweighed any other con-cerns for the present time. The spring semester looked even more promising than the one just ended, at least socially.

"Do you really want to go into medicine Victor?" asked a stern Dr. Grant, Victor's academic advisor for his pre-med program.

"Well, I was always pretty good at biology and it seems interesting . . ."

Dr. Grant quickly followed this rather weak statement of intent with a rundown of Victor's even weaker grades the past semester.

"Victor, aptitude and potential are wonderful things, but they have to translate into results. Did you know that sixty percent of pre-med freshman end up doing something else?"

Victor, not quite sure if this was a rhetorical question, just nodded his head in acknowledgment.

"Victor, the fact of the matter is that we have a limited number of seats available in this department for pre-med. It's a competitive major. A lot of young people want to become doctors."

Again Victor nodded, feeling increasingly ill at ease with the direction this talk was taking.

"Look, I can't justify allowing you to stay in the program with these grades. I'm going to have to put you on academic probation for next semester. Everything that is C has to come up to B, but the real problem is the D's and F's. They have to come up to a C; and remember, no medical college is going to look at you with a C average. You'll have to have at least a B average by your senior year."

"Okay." Victor managed to say in a tone that was much more optimistic than he felt. "I understand, Dr. Grant. I know I can do it if I just focus."

"Yes, I'm sure you can," said Dr. Grant, grateful to have reached the end of the conversation.

He would be able to write in his file that a warning had been issued. Along with the letter Victor had already been sent, the inevitable end of the young man's pre-med aspirations was no longer his concern.

Victor left the handsome 19th century brick townhouse which housed the biology administration, with its high ceilings and ornate moldings, the legacy of the town's great coal barons, feeling oddly relieved. Deep down he knew his current entertainment enterprise was at odds with any chance of making it to medical school. Now that the prospect of leaving the program was placed before him, he realized that he didn't even mind. Who wanted to be a doctor anyway? They worked crazy hours and were confronted by the sick and dying. His father's business seemed downright pleasant in comparison. At least those people were dead, not gasping physical wrecks looking at him to halt the inevitable. Perhaps he could become an accountant or school teacher. The course work would be easier and the job much more pleasant. By the time he reached his door, Victor was riding a new wave of optimism.

You're only young once, and if you waste it now you can't come back later and retrieve these days of freedom and glory, he mused to himself.

And so Victor's second semester at Wilkes wasn't really any better than the first. For one thing, he was forced to space out his parties so as not to run afoul of Sophie's narrowing tolerance. There was always the nagging thought that maybe he should turn over a new leaf and actually spend a couple hours some nights studying. But Victor fundamentally lacked the ability to sacrifice for long term goals. Clever as he was, he was a 'carpe diem' sort of guy. Vic could lose himself in many ways. There was television, listening to music, phone calls, a little pot, and yes dates with some of the girls. Time passes quickly when you are having fun. Just as the weather was breaking with sunny days and new life all around outside, Victor had to face the end of the second semester. He still had no idea what he was going to do with his life, but it seems others did.

Dr. Grant, in an even shorter meeting than the last time, told Victor matter-of-factly that he was out of biology and pre-med. He could switch to another major, Dr. Grant suggested sociology or psychology, and reapply to the program if his grades improved. In this scenario, Victor would be unlikely to graduate within four years, but that wasn't a problem for the school.

When Victor saw his father's car out front to pick him up for Easter break, he mentally reviewed how he would sell his change of heart about going to med school. By the time his slid into the passenger's seat, he felt fairly confident, that is until he heard his father's cheerful greeting.

"And how's Dr. Kozol doing this fine spring morning!"

"I'm not a doctor yet, Dad!" Victor managed as the car left the city headed for Route 81, the highway that ran northeast towards Duryea.

After asking about his father and the business (good, plenty of business, i.e., death), Victor decided to work in his main objective for this trip; convince his father that flunking out of the pre-med program was a lifestyle choice and great career move.

"You know, Dad, one of the reasons I really wanted to be a doctor was to help people."

"Sure, Victor, that's a nice motivation."

"But, in today's world a lot of people have more mental and emotional problems. I think I might be more interested in helping people this way."

"What, like as a psychiatrist?"

"I was thinking of something more in the line of therapy. I've been reading a lot about it."

"Yah, but you don't need to go to medical school for that stuff."

"I guess that's it. I'm thinking of switching my major to psychology."

"What! Why even go to college! You'll never get a job with that!"

"That's not true, Dad. There are lots of ways you can apply a psychology degree."

"I don't know, in today's economy . . ."

In the back of Victor's father's mind, he had resigned himself to Victor running the family business after all. And who was to say that psychology wouldn't be a good way to prepare for it. At least the boy would have a college degree.

Nothing was said to Victor's mother over the Easter weekend filled with her famous scalloped potatoes, ham, and pickled red beets. Victor's sister came home for the holiday and Victor was only too happy for the distraction.

Vic finished up the semester ingloriously by having failed only one course, biochemistry. Of this Victor was proud. Since he lived in an apartment and not a student dorm, staying in Wilkes-Barre for the summer was not a problem. Victor found a job at a local market.

So Vic went back to Wilkes, and as a sophomore was able to stay in school as a C student, but he knew he would never get back into pre-med. So he did what he always does, he went back to periods of lethargy punctuated by bursts of energy in throwing and attending parties. Vic realized he had to be more careful because Sophie was always vigilant from her downstairs perch. He knows the days she went to her sister for a visit and schedules his affairs accordingly. Vic actually skated through two more years of college this way. But it was the end of his junior year when things came to a head. Vic was spending even less time in a major he really had no interest in. His grade point average plummeted to below a D and Vic was on his way to being finished at Wilkes.

If this wasn't bad enough, someone left the water running in the tub during a party, which was full of ice and beer. It overflowed and started to leak down into Sophie's apartment. By the time it was noticed, a section of her kitchen ceiling collapsed into two trays of pirogies she had just made. Sophie ordered Vic and his roommate out, but only after presenting him with a bill for $2,000 to replace a section of the ceiling and clean up the mess. How to keep this dual disaster from his father was going to be the greatest challenge of Vic's life.

The Family Business

VICTOR'S FATHER ALBERT was sitting on his back porch admiring the wonderful summer scenes and taking in the fresh air all around him. But his thoughts were elsewhere; he was thinking back eighty years when his grandfather, Stanislas Kozlowski came to America to work in the then booming coal mines in northeast Pennsylvania. His son Stanley, who liked to be called Stash, shortened the family name to Kozol and began working for an undertaker (as funeral directors were called back then). He found life in the sunlight infinitely better than the dangerous and unhealthy working conditions of the mines. In the winter, the only time miners saw daylight was on Sunday; it was dark when they left for the mines and dark when they came home. "Now that's depressing," thought Albert.

Stash was married but with his wife working, he was able to save enough for the tuition to attend an eight week course in Philadelphia at the Eckles College of Mortuary Science. After that he officially registered as an apprentice to the undertaker he was working with for two years. Finally, he took the test and was awarded a license to practice undertaking in the Commonwealth of Pennsylvania. When his mentor, Stanley Sipkovich, retired in 1932 Stash put out his own shingle and became the official Polish undertaker for Duryea.

Even though it was the middle of The Great Depression, Stash had supported his family of four children quite well; they were raised in middle class surroundings. He had the added benefit of being looked up to as a needed professional in his town. Stash sent two of his sons to four-year colleges, his daughter married, and his third son, Albert, followed his father into Eckles Mortuary Science School in Philadelphia to become what is now called a funeral director. It was Albert who was to first help in and finally take over the family business. The Kozols, in 1939, moved into a retired doctor's mansion and remodeled the first floor into what was now a funeral home. The upstairs was the apartment for the family.

This expansion was necessary as people no longer held open casket viewings of their deceased relatives in their living rooms, but rather at the local funeral home. After serving three years in the U.S. Army during World War II, Albert returned home to partner with his father in the business.

Albert was a smoother, more polished version of his father since he had a high school education and one-year at Eckles. He was an active member of Holy Rosary Polish Catholic Church, and also donated to the neighboring Polish National Church and other churches. Albert was in The Knights of Columbus, Kiwanis, Veterans of Foreign Wars, American Legion, and served on the library board. Funeral directors were known to be great 'joiners'. So, when it was time for his father to retire, Albert was more than ready to seamlessly continue the decades old family business. By doing so Albert was able to hold on to his core business and add some new families.

However, since Duryea during this period went from 10,000 to 6,000, the business was now doing sixty funerals per year down from a high of seventy in Stash's heyday. But, Kozol's was still the largest funeral home in town, since the other two directors had also lost business due to population declines.

Albert ran the funeral home from the mid-fifties until the eighties when it was time to begin thinking of the transition of ownership to a new generation. He now had to think of what was to become of his only son after the debacle at Wilkes. Albert decided to give an ultimatum to Vic meeting the problem head-on.

"Vic, you either go downstate to mortuary school in Bethlehem and get a funeral director's license, or I am going to sell the business, retire, and you can 'paddle your own canoe' from there."

Joining the family business was not a prospect that thrilled Vic, but he was astute enough to know that his options could be worse. To refuse his father's offer would put him on the street looking for work with no marketable skills. This usually meant minimum wage type employment. A job so tiring and boring, you won't want to party after your shift is over. Imagine, standing at the local hot dog joint window with your white hat asking people all day, "Do you want yours plain or with mustard?" This was a real bummer to contemplate. Victor was trapped, he needed money and his father was no longer going to just give it to him.

Vic had two cousins downstate. One was a cardiologist practicing in a large hospital in Philadelphia, and the other was an orthopedic specialist practicing with a group in Allentown. This was no longer possible for Vic, no matter how much he yearned for the more exciting greener pastures down state, he had screwed up and he knew it.

CHAPTER 4

A New Beginning

VIC HAD TO get busy if he hoped to not lose any more time getting into his new career. While the Northampton County Area Community College Funeral Service program was not attended by rocket scientists, it was a heavily science oriented curriculum. Vic didn't have any science courses of C or better to transfer. None of his D's or F's were acceptable, so he had to take a full load of science courses at summer school at the Luzerne County Community College in Nanticoke. He still wouldn't be able to graduate in one year. It would take eighteen months for Vic to get the ordinary twelve month diploma, because the other students already had an education of mostly science courses in their first two years of college. Three years of education was the Pennsylvania requirement. This inability to transfer many of his college credits was the cause for much distress for Vic.

Whether, he was getting older or was just tired from all of the partying in Wilkes-Barre, Vic was a quieter, more sober student in Bethlehem; not that he didn't drink on weekends. He no longer hosted parties. If anything, Vic went from motivated to do the wrong things, to just plain apathetic about himself and his future. He was able to keep average grades in school this time, realizing he really wanted to get all of this behind him and start making money.

Finally, in January the day arrived for Vic's mid-year graduation from funeral school. His parents sat proudly in the front row as their son strode across the stage with cameras clicking and people applauding. Pennsylvania, like most States require an internship working with a funeral director for an additional year after graduation before taking the State Board Exams and being awarded a license.

Technically, Vic's father could have been the 'preceptor' for Vic, but Albert chose to call his good friend Charley Rokowski in Scranton to take his son on. Charley did twice the business that Vic's father did in Duryea. There, he would get his much needed experience. Earning $200.00 per week, Vic spent the year helping direct funerals and embalm bodies in Scranton.

Finally, Vic had free time to hit the bars once again. He would get mildly buzzed and go back to his room over the funeral home garage in downtown Scranton.

With the year finally over, Vic made the trek to Philadelphia and took his state boards. In another month he was notified by registered letter that he has passed all requirements and was officially a licensed funeral director in the great state of Pennsylvania.

It had been six years since Vic first entered Wilkes University, and he finally had something to show for all of this time. *Not to mention tens of thousands of his father's money.* Vic was not ecstatic; this was not his chosen field, but rather a fall-back or default career. He didn't relish working for his father, but as he reasoned earlier, doing unskilled labor would be far worse.

Funeral Directing in a Small Town

VIC WASN'T EXCITED to return to Duryea to live full-time after having been away for six years. Most of Vic's high school friends who remained behind married early and were settled into the service industry jobs that still existed. Vic feared he would appear like an alien to his old friends after being away so long.

He now lived five miles from the spot near Pittston, where in 1957 the Susquehanna River broke through into a mine tunnel located too close to the river. Most of the miners miraculously escaped with their lives, but the gaping hole poured millions of gallons of water into the mine. Since the mines were all interconnected, all of the deep mines in Luzerne County were permanently flooded. This disaster ended the last of the deep mining of anthracite in the area. Strip mining continued on a smaller scale, but the markets for this form of energy were not to return.

The federal, state, and local governments poured millions of dollars into the area to try and diversify the industrial base. At first this seemed to help, but then low-wage states down south and cheap overseas labor closed many of these new factories. To keep coal alive, Congress was induced to pass legislation that named anthracite coal as the primary heating fuel for military and other governmental buildings. However, nothing could ever replace the thousands of miners' jobs now long gone in northeast Pennsylvania. Some businesses found niches and prospered, and the colleges, hospitals, governmental facilities and other institutions in the area did go on and provide a steady source of employment for a smaller labor force. Vic knew that there would not be growth in his area and he couldn't, in his lifetime, remember when the area was humming with tens of thousands employed by the mines.

Victor's parents bought a modest ranch home three miles out of town in Pittston Township, and moved out of the apartment on top of the funeral home. With some leftover furniture from his grandmother, Vic moved into the family manor where he grew up. Working with his father every day was actually easy, because Albert made all of the decisions and Vic was the schlepper. He removed and embalmed bodies, took folding chairs to the widow's houses, washed cars, hosed off the porches, ran the vacuum, and in short did all of the trivial, and some of the important details, needed to keep the funeral home running smoothly.

To successfully operate a sixty call a year business in a small town, you might spend two weeks with no funerals and then have three deaths in two days, requiring you to put in an eighty hour week to get it all done. This is where the expression 'feast or famine' came from.

As to the public relations part of the business; Vic was weak in that department. He was seen in church only when doing funerals. Rarely did he attend the other important events like suppers, carnivals, socials, and oh yes, the annual bowling banquets. Then came the block parties, 4th of July parades, and all sorts of local events the funeral director was expected to either attend or help run. All of this mingling was with people who were twice to three times his age. Not to mention the expectations that you not be a womanizer or ever appear drunk in public.

These were the things Albert could do seamlessly and even seemed to enjoy; but to Vic, this stuff was torture and a waste of time. Albert got tired of cajoling Vic into talking his place in the town and its activities. He knew this was a weakness with his son, but just as in college, he seemed to have no control over Victor when it came to changing behavior. So, a standoff ensued. Albert was satisfied to have Vic did the physical work around the funeral home, while he would remain the public relations person. This agreement worked well while Albert stayed active in the business, but was to have disastrous consequences down the road. For the time being, Victor was making $20,000 a year, had a car to use, and a place to stay. Maybe not Vic's idea of a road to greatness, but he wasn't wanting for anything.

CHAPTER 6

Victor the Proprietor

AFTER FIVE YEARS of this monotonous existence, things were about to change. Albert and Mary's best friends the Chulak's retired from their flower shop and moved to Ft. Lauderdale, Florida. They invited the Kozols down for a vacation, and they became hooked on the balmy climate and laid back lifestyle being lived by their friends. Steve Chulak told Albert that there was a nice little condo nearby coming up for sale by a lady who went to a nursing home. Albert and Mary made an appointment to see it, fell in love with the place and quickly agreed to buy it.

They return to Duryea, and the next Monday meet with Vic to tell him they had decided to retire to Florida. Victor would be the boss at last! He was taken aback by this sudden change of roles with his father, but it did give him more freedom. Among the many conditions and stipulations in the agreement that Victor had to sign with his father, was the one where he would have to send his parents $3,000 a month as rent for the business and building. After all of this and a warning from his father that he would no longer be there to backstop the public relations end of the business. Vic assured Albert that things would be different, now that he is in charge. By the end of the summer, the older Kozols were gone and Victor was finally his own boss.

Victor's First Year in Business

ONCE AGAIN, VIC made resolution that he was going to be different and make this work. But, alone and with no one to criticize his actions or lack thereof, he fell prey to the same apathy that he was prone to at college.

He handled the funerals when they came in, but the client families could tell his heart wasn't in it. The bodies he put out on display for public viewings didn't look as good as the ones displayed by his competitors. The place wasn't as clean or maintained as well as it used to be, and worse Vic would sometimes be drunk in town within view of his clients. (In funeral service parlance, the 'client families' are the next of kin left behind when someone dies, they are the real customers.)

With two other active competitors in a town of only 6,000 people Vic couldn't afford to alienate many families and stay in business. If he disappointed and angered enough of his client families they will soon put out the word "don't call Victor," when in need of a funeral service.

This was the beginning of a year from hell that would propel him into a downward spiral. Vic's first year in business was a series of blunders and embarrassments. Instead of working for his father and drawing $400.00 per week, for the first time in his life, he was untethered from the mother ship. If he screwed up this business, there would be no guaranteed income; in fact there may be no income at all, and that was a scary thought for Vic.

But for all of his life, Vic never had to put duty before pleasure, and he was finding it hard to do it now. Many people who start their own businesses fail because they lose the rigor and discipline of an organization that used to employ them. They just don't self-motivate. Vic, was never really motivated working for his father and this weakness carried over into his newfound freedom of making his own schedule and lifestyle. Vic kept falling farther into the abyss.

After receiving a call from an, old mortuary school friend from Bethlehem, Vic said no to an invite downstate. But after two more friends called him and told him what a good reunion he would be missing if he didn't attend this one in New Hope, Vic finally caved in and when Friday afternoon came, he left for Bucks County to knock a few back with his old college chums.

When funeral directors want to take time off, like doctors, they have to find someone to fill in for them in case an emergency comes up while they are away. However, Victor wasn't on any kind of terms with any other local directors, so he took the chance that someone wouldn't die at home while he was away. (If they died in a hospital or nursing home, you had time to pick up the body later, but at home you had to go immediately.)

When the answering service rang Vic's cell phone he was in a bar in New Hope some three hours' drive from home. The problem was that the deceased Mrs. Makovsky was lying on her face in the kitchen after she suffered an apparent heart attack. The children were gathered in the living room one room away from their dead mother; they had just met with the family doctor who had pronounced her dead and told them to call a funeral director to remove the body. For over fifty years the Kozol's had taken care of deaths in the Makovsky family; this funeral was to be no different. To have a family call someone else you would really have to make a negative impression on them, after they used your firm for generations. This is how Vic's worse nightmare came true; he was hours away from Duryea and only a seventy- year-old handyman who would be incapable of removing the body alone was left back in Duryea. Victor called the family and lied that he was out on another death call and "won't be able to get there for a while." Victor had no way of knowing at the time that he wasn't going to get there at all.

After hastily saying his goodbyes to his friends, Vic took the two lane roads through rural Bucks County at high speed. It was now midnight and the roads were nearly empty. Just as he was approaching the Quakertown interchange of the Pennsylvania Turnpike, Vic couldn't believe it when the red and blue lights he was seeing in his rear view mirror were getting closer. Within a minute the State trooper was alongside and signaling him to pull over. Vic had an expired insurance card and no registration card for the vehicle he was driving, and he reeked of alcohol. The only worse thing to get you to spend the night in a local jail would be to run someone over.

Meanwhile back in Duryea, the Makovskys could no longer reach Vic on his cell phone, and his answering service had no idea where he was. In disgust, with their mother turning blue, they call Jake Borovich another local funeral director to remove their mother. Within thirty minutes their mother was out of the house and Borovich was sitting in the kitchen with the family making the arrangements.

The next morning Vic's friend Steve Lamont, a local attorney wired the money and got Vic sprung from the Quakertown Police holding cell. Now Vic is $500.00 poorer, has a hangover, and was facing a court hearing later for additional punishment which would include the near certainty of losing his driving license if convicted of a DUI. It could be worse, the people in Duryea don't read downstate newspapers and the event didn't get published in the Wilkes-Barre papers. However, this is all Vic would be able to salvage from his night of partying.

At least Vic didn't attend Holy Rosary, the local Polish Catholic Church (or any other) so he never had to hear in person the rumors buzzing around how he never came to pick up the body of the president of the Altar and Rosary Society after her untimely death at the age of eighty four.

Victor could have billed that funeral out at about $4,000 (depending on the merchandise chosen). After the cemetery, church, merchandise, and other miscellaneous costs, he could have grossed about $2,000. The fixed costs of maintaining the funeral are there anyway. So, the final profit would be less. However this funeral would have mostly paid his father the rent for the current month.

Vic not only lost the Makovsky funeral, he had a way of compounding his problems without ever planning it. When the daughter of another client family was killed in a tragic auto accident, in which the driver was her drunken boyfriend. After attending a party in Wilkes-Barre where he drank too much, Ted was driving Lisa home and missed a turn on River Road plunging down an embankment and finally hitting a large oak tree which prevented the car from landing in the Susquehanna River. Ted had only minor injuries but the tree hit was on the right side of Ted's Camaro coupe. Lisa, at only eighteen, was killed instantly. All of this made the nerves and emotions of the family much more sensitive than with a natural death.

In making the arrangements with the Tibursky family, Vic was given one admonition by the dead girl's father, "Under no circumstances are you to let that drunken, no good SOB into the funeral home to see Lisa's body."

Vic knew Ted Chernowski, the driver and boyfriend involved, from high school days. The next night while having a drink in Tubby's a local hangout, Vic was approached by Ted now out on bail. Ted asked one favor *for old times' sake*. Could he see his girlfriend one last time? Vic initially said no, but two drinks later and after more badgering by Ted, he relented.

Chapter 7

"Only if you swear to me that this will be a secret just between us."

"Of course," Ted swore. So, Vic drove him to the funeral home at midnight to have the private viewing in his morgue. All went well with the Lisa Tibursky funeral until a week later. Ted was back at Tubby's drinking and boasting that he never liked Lisa's old man (the feeling was mutual; as he tried to break up the relationship many times, but his daughter had turned eighteen and wouldn't stop seeing Ted) but that he had the last laugh; he had influence with a friend Vic, that got him in to see Lisa for the last time before her funeral. He was even circulating a picture of Lisa under a white sheet on the morgue table. When the news got back to Lisa parents they were so enraged they refused to pay the funeral bill and threatened a lawsuit for damages. They also threatened to report Vic to the State Board of Funeral Directors for unethical practices.

Another $4,500 was now in jeopardy and Vic was furious. He called his lawyer Steve Lamont and recounted "I did all of this work for them and the funeral went off very well and now they don't want to pay me, this is nuts."

Three days later Lamont phoned back but the news was bleak for Vic. If the State Board called a formal hearing in Harrisburg, Vic could face sanctions. They could tell Vic to disavow the bill all or in part; they could fine him separately; and they could suspend his license for an indeterminate amount of time. The news got worse; they would publish the hearing findings in the local newspapers. Steve's advice to Vic was to write off the funeral bill and apologize to the Tibursky family.

Circling the Drain

WITH A YEAR going for him like this, Victor found himself in the worst financial condition of his short career. The refrain in the town "Don't call Vic", was taking its toll on Vic's checkbook. His normal checking reserves of $6,000 had fallen to below $3,000. From this he owed his parents $3,000 not to mention the utilities, taxes and other expenses of keeping the place going. He also needed something to live on.

It worried Vic enough that he even contemplated playing the role of his father and grandfather before him. Attend church, volunteer for the bazaars and even ride the rubber chicken circuit of the bowling banquets. However, these were all long range plans, and Victor needed cash now. Vic did what he always did in a crisis, nothing. He slid back into a stupor and became mostly invisible in Duryea. And yes, the business continued to decline to only twenty-five funerals per year average. This was down more than half of what he started with.

Immediate action had to be taken, or his parents would soon know that he had failed them when the next check didn't arrive. Victor then called the two local banks in Duryea and got an appointment to see the commercial loan officers. After reviewing Vic's books the message was the same from both bankers. You do not have sufficient assets, cash flow, and collateral to justify a line of credit for your business. In a final desperate move Vic thought of Randy Simcoe, a classmate who made it big with cable TV franchising. So, he called Randy and explained his plight.

Randy was comforting and interested in Vic's situation, but he had invested all of his reserves in another venture and couldn't get at them at this time. Vic got the message and knew that he was on his own. He alone would have to come up with a solution to his problem.

He had to try everything before he gave up. Victor went to the corner convenience store and bought $400 worth of Pennsylvania lottery tickets at one time. After scoring a minor $50 hit, he was now behind $350. Vic mused, for one number I could have won $5,000 instead of $50, I'm getting close. The next night he got in his car and drove to the Mohegan Sun Casino outside Wilkes-Barre to try his luck on a larger scale. After hitting at blackjack on two separate nights for a total of $3,000, Vic had a major setback on the third night and lost $4,000.

Vic yelled at himself in the car going home, "I was so close to winning another month's respite; so close!"

With options closing for him at home, Vic needed to try one more thing. Finally, as one last desperate move, Vic packed up the car and headed for Atlantic City; the Vegas of the East. He still had his credit cards and he needed to make just one big score. If he got $6,000 ahead he could leave and call it a victory.

On a Friday night Victor arrived at Bally's, a casino on the boardwalk. He checked in. Forgoing supper, he hit the tables. Luck finally turned in Vic's favor and by midnight he was up $5,000. Tired from the three-and-a-half hour drive, he decided to turn in and make his final 'withdrawal' the next night. But, Saturday was not to be a repeat of Friday. By 11:00 p.m. Vic was down $6,000 and he started to hit the booze harder. By 1:00 a.m. Vic was down $10,000, the five he won yesterday plus five more in the hole. All of it was gone. He sat despondent at the bar in a cocktail lounge next to the blackjack tables drowning his sorrows. Just then, a well-dressed man, maybe a few years older than Vic, took a seat next to him. The stranger looked over at Vic, "You had a bad night at the tables too?"

Victor sullenly nodded and figures misery must love company. By 3:00 a.m. Vic knows his new friend is Sam, an attorney from New York City. Victor tells Sam his sad life story, but Sam stays sketchy on any details of his life.

One thing leads to another and Sam says, "Do you ever watch any of the crime shows on TV?"

Vic responds, "I always liked Law and Order."

Sam responds, "Yes, and that show is a good example of all of the forensic science available to the police; it's getting harder and harder to get away with murder."

"You're right, I know of cases back home where bodies are exhumed years later and enough DNA and other evidence is left to convict someone who thought they got away with murder."

Sam responded, "That's the problem for the bad guys, unless you atomize the body, it's still there to be found and analyzed far into the future."

Vic says, "The closest thing to atomizing a body is to cremate it."

"How so?" Sam asks.

"Look, you take a 200 pound body and in two hours at 1,600 degrees Fahrenheit, the body is reduced to a pound or two of bone fragments, no larger than gravel, when finally pulverized in a grinding machine; which is used so that the remains fit into an urn."

Sam says, "You mean you could never tell who the ashes belonged to, not even with DNA testing?"

"That's the way I read it, in fact all states have laws that delay a cremation for a day or two after death so that a coroner or medical examiner can order an autopsy if they feel it necessary to investigate the manner of death of the deceased. They don't want the body destroyed before they can get a chance to look at it, because after the cremation any possible investigation is over."

"Very interesting . . . say Vic, do you do cremations at your funeral home?"

"No, we are too small of an operation, so we farm them out to a nearby cemetery that has a retort to do them for us."

Sam responds, "Just how involved is a cremation?

Victor, remembering his seminar at funeral service school, goes into his dialogue.

"Cremation ovens used to be like large bakery ovens, but are now more compact and lower in price say about $50,000. In fact they are about the size of a car and are delivered by truck fully assembled and usually slid right into position in the intended building. You then wire up, hook up the natural gas and presto you are in the cremation business. But perhaps I am oversimplifying. There are permits and other considerations, but the cost and a garage sized space would be the most significant. Of course, if you need to build a structure for the retort it would cost a lot more; and this is what the cemetery we use has." Vic further elaborates, "It would not be feasible to install a crematory with his size business, even though more and more people are choosing this method of disposal each year. The wholesale charge for a cremation (like we pay the cemetery) is say $300; the retail to the families is about twice that much. Now you see how many cases it would take to pay back the initial investment."

Sam responded, "Suppose someone did cremations for a select market and paid $10,000 for each case."

"Sure, it would change the case numbers downward drastically, but who would ever pay that when they can get it for far less anywhere else?"

"It depends."

"No matter, I couldn't front the money for a retort anyway."

"That's what I do for a living, I work with venture capitalists. We front the costs for startup or expanding businesses because there may be a special opportunity that a conventional bank might overlook."

"Yes, but too good to be true in my case."

With some final small talk, the two new friends take leave of each other exchanging business cards and promising to stay in touch in the future.

Aftermath of Atlantic City

MONDAY, AFTER THE debacle of Atlantic City, Victor is back in Duryea. It has been three weeks without a funeral, his credit cards are nearly maxed out, and his checkbook balance is all but nonexistent.

"Should I just walk out?" Victor thinks out loud.

Giving the keys back to his father and quitting would be the quickest way to end the pain. But for now, Vic decided once again to put off any hard choices and does nothing. He hopes that just one funeral coming in the door right now would make a payment to his father and buy him some time. But unfortunately, he can't create this business by running a sale like some retailer would do. He has to wait patiently.

Back in New York City, Sam Gianetti, the attorney with mob connections that Victor mysteriously met in Atlantic City is sitting at his desk and reflecting on his life.

Sam remembers growing up in Plainfield New Jersey. It was a middle class neighborhood with tree lined streets dotted with modest ranch houses. Sam's dad was a machinist at the local

Mack diesel engine plant. Sam's mother was a secretary for a local attorney. Many times, over the years, he heard stories from his mother about the more interesting parts of the law. Some of the cases were as if they were from a screenplay on TV. They were real with people you could identify with. He also found that, by the time he reached high school, he had an aptitude for the social sciences and English.

After graduation, Sam applied and was accepted in pre-law at Rutgers, the State University of New Jersey. After graduating in four years, he was accepted into Rutgers Law School and graduated with honors three years later. Now, Sam, like so many recent law graduates, headed to the Big Apple across the Hudson River to find employment.

The first job he lands is as an Associate at Carmine Associates in Queens, New York. While not a 'mob' connected firm, they did have a client who had a brother who was connected. The firm agreed to defend one Mario DeSilva on a drug distribution rap. As the new lawyer on staff, Sam drew the straw to defend Mario. Sam handled the case well, but got lucky when the key prosecution witness against Mario couldn't be found to testify. Mario was consequently acquitted of all charges in a short two day trial. What Sam didn't know was that Mario was a 'soldier' for the Dellveccio organization, and that Carlo Dellveccio, the Don of the family, was watching the court proceedings with great interest.

Carlo called Sam a week after the trial and set up a meeting at Carlo's office in Brooklyn. Carlo's office is down by the docks and is a commercial garbage hauling company. "DeLorenzo and Sons" is the name on the door of the old redbrick three-story warehouse. He was directed up a narrow steel staircase to a mezzanine area overlooking the large truck garage below. However, after entering a glass framed door, Sam was in a very well-decorated formal office suite. A well-dressed and good looking secretary, probably in her fifties, told Sam to follow her to Mr. DellVeccio's office. It was a large oak paneled room with a beautiful multi-colored Persian rug and other very expensive furnishings to match.

"Good to meet you at last, Sam."

With this, Carlo asked Sam to be seated on a large crimson leather sofa. After exchanging pleasantries with this very urbane and pleasant person, he felt at ease. After a discussion about Sam's depth in criminal and civil legal proceedings, Carlo made Sam an offer. He was to start up his own practice in Brooklyn and would be given all of the set-up money he need to have an independent law firm.

It was agreed that Sam would bill Carlo for all work done at $300 an hour with a guarantee minimum of $150,000 a year. In addition Sam would receive $100,000 a year for office expenses, a secretary, and any other things that he may need. The only stipulation was that Sam had to agree that Carlo, or anyone he designates, would be the only clients Sam would take.

The package offered was more than twice what he earned as an Associate at Carmines, where raises will be much slower coming and moving up would take years; if you even get promoted at all. There are also too many lawyers in circulation, so promotions would be slow coming in any other law firm.

Carlo's 'other' operations need a business manager, and Sam would have a future there with an even larger salary for operating the legal part of Carlo's underworld operations. (It should be noted here that while the mob does many things off-the-books with drugs, prostitution, and gambling, they also are involved in legitimate businesses. These are necessary to operate so that they can launder money generated from their illegal operations.)

The mob owns, through straw purchasers: laundries, restaurants, trucking companies, garbage disposal firms, and many other businesses. All of these need legal representation and business management. This was a tough decision for Sam; he held no illusions that he was dealing with a branch of the mob. But, he rationalized that he would be dealing with just the legal and criminal defense portions of their business, not the illegal stuff under the surface. And Sam thought Carlo might be more of a modern day Don cutting loose the old, crude illegal operations like you see on TV and concentrating on the legal businesses. He had thought, that's why he wants a business manager, right?

Deep down Sam knew that once you became ensnared with an organization like Dellveccio's, you don't just walk away. But Sam was under thirty, unattached and living in pretty rundown quarters in a small efficiency in a downtrodden neighborhood in Queens. He could really see himself living in a modern condo in the right neighborhood with a shiny new set of wheels in the garage underneath. No more fast food, and Chinese takeout, he could dine in posh restaurants, and maybe meet a suitable partner along the way. Sam did the math and was sold; he will be Dellveccio's *mouthpiece*.

It is three years later, and Sam is sitting in his office with the Brooklyn Bridge framed out his office window, reviewing a case that he is fully involved in for his employer. One Bruno Albino is two years after the fact being accused of murdering a police informant. Why is this happening now so long after the event? It's because on a suspicion of finding new evidence, the State exhumed and autopsied the body of a Joe DeSilva for a second time. With new and advanced spectroscopic testing it was found that Desilva's body had residues of the same lethal compound in it that was found in Bruno's kitchen. In updating Carlo, Sam relayed this information over the phone.

Carlo responded "I thought we were past this situation after the original investigation turned up nothing?"

"The problem is Carlo, Sam says, that in murder cases there is no statute of limitations."

If only the body had just disappeared instead of being buried. Now Sam has to resurrect the case and mount a defense to try to get Bruno off. After all, Bruno is very effective at what he does and has whacked three more people since killing DeSilva. To lose his talent would be a blow to the organization. And, there is always the risk of Bruno taking a plea and singing to the authorities. If this doesn't give a mob lawyer a migraine, what will?

Sam has an organizational meeting tonight, and will just have to level with the others about Bruno's chances in court. If Sam says the odds are against Bruno, he could lose influence with his peers. If he guarantees an acquittal and doesn't deliver in court, it would be even worse. Would they find another mouthpiece? Who knows? That's why in any criminal law practice there is always risk, but with the organization the risks are of an infinitely greater magnitude. Sam has eight hours to fine tune his report for the meeting.

The Dinner Meeting

IT'S 8:00 P.M. in the rear dining room at Rosselli's, which is by the way a very fine Italian restaurant in Brooklyn that caters (up-front) to tourists and locals alike. The restaurant is operated by a very fine chef who hails from Sicily.

Luigi Rosselli is a tenant of the Dellveccio family that actually owns the building and equipment through a straw purchaser. The rear of the restaurant is the other Rosselli's that the public doesn't get to see. The walls are paneled in fine dark walnut and oriental carpets cover the inlaid teak flooring. There are brass accents, and classical Italian paintings on the wall. The 'club room' has a beautiful mahogany table set with Irish linen and German silverware with place settings for twelve. Here the family, a group of twelve men from their thirties to their seventies, is assembled. The aroma of pasta with a sauce simmered for hours wafts from the table. Fine French and Italian wine flows freely, and the talk around the table is jovial and light hearted. If you're going to gorge yourself on fine Italian food right through the antipasto, pasta, veal, and cannoli, this is the place to do it.

Everyone knows the business meeting is about to begin when the plates are cleared and the Havana cigars are broken out. Carlo

Dellveccio is seventy two years old, meticulously dressed in a Brooks Brothers navy blue pin striped suit befitting any captain of industry; not to mention that his Rolex, diamond cuff links, and ring are also impeccable. This is Carlo, the Don and undisputed head of this family.

After listening patiently to all of the routine monthly reports of revenue and expenses, Carlo gets to new business. This is always the most interesting part of every meeting. Under legal issues, Sam has to address the problem of Bruno Albino's recent arrest.

All eyes are on Sam who says, "Because of the solid forensic evidence, the chances of an acquittal are less than fifty-percent."

This is not what the eleven others wanted to hear, but after spending the entire afternoon reviewing similar cases, Sam can't say anything more positive. This forces Carlo to have to do damage control. If convicted, it will mean offering a large payout to Bruno's wife and children, who will have to wait patiently for him while he is serving a possibly lengthy prison term upstate. This does not count the tens of thousands of dollars for Bruno's defense and appeals. No business likes to take profits already booked from deals long closed and have to give them back later. It was ugly, but Sam had to say it now, because if he promised an acquittal and it didn't happen, things would certainly be nasty for him.

After this unpleasantness is dealt with, the main business portion of the meeting is closed. Next Carlo successively points to each of his men around the room querying each for their observations and suggestions regarding various business issues. When it is Sam's turn he recounts his chance meeting last weekend in Atlantic City with a young funeral director from Pennsylvania. He tells his associates about the wonderful world of cremating bodies; leaving no trace for the authorities to sniff around analyzing later.

"Not now or ever," Sam recounts. "Consider the case of Jimmy Hoffa. For thirty years there have been theories as to what happened to him, his body, or if he is even dead. But, like you read in crime novels, no "corpus delicti", no case. If Joe DeSilva's body had been cremated two years ago, we wouldn't be facing this expensive and time consuming problem today."

Sam goes even further out on the limb with his next statement. "What if we owned or had use of our own crematory? We would be able to get rid of these inconvenient pieces of evidence permanently and completely. We obviously won't be able to dispose of every body, particularly if the hit was done in public. But, if the hits are carried out privately in remote areas, we could take care of these bodies with cremation."

Sam continues, "Think of all the effort and risk we take trying to bury bodies in cement to weigh them down in the bay. We know our friends in the garbage rackets have put many bodies in landfills, but even here there is the risk that even a small trace can be found and subjected to increasingly sophisticated analysis, DNA being only one example. Hell, there is even a case where some bozos rented a tree chipping machine and ground up a body, oblivious to the fact that they were splattering traceable DNA samples throughout the machine and surroundings, which provided plenty of DNA samples for a conviction. On the other hand, cremation is neat, clean, and permanent."

Carlo tells Sam, "Look, it seems far-fetched, but if we could pull this off there would be a lot less defense work for you in the future Sam. You might even be putting yourself out of a job (chuckles). Look into the matter and report back as to its feasibility for us next meeting."

Sam says, "Okay, and we'll code name the project 'firestop.' Meeting adjourned."

Reflecting

THE NEXT MORNING Sam is once again back in his corner office with his picture perfect view of the Brooklyn Bridge and the Manhattan skyline. But the beautiful day outside is far from his mind. He is thinking about how far he has come in three years. He had risen from a lawyer at the bottom of the ladder in a large firm, to being his own boss of a tony law practice catering to a mob family. Once on-board, Sam could never look back. With all of the perks and easy living, has come tremendous responsibilities. To say that the criminal side of his work is a matter of life and death is not an overstatement.

The organization Sam is fronting for relies on his judgment, connections, and sometimes high wire acts to survive. The family needs the authorities as far from their enterprises as can be managed at all times. Sam has to throw up as many legal delays and roadblocks as possible. On the civil law side, he is buying and selling properties, laundering and investing millions of dollars in places as close as New York and as far away as Switzerland and the Cayman Islands.

Among his many duties he defends against lawsuits and negotiates leases and deals for the many legitimate businesses they operate. The one thing that is different from regular law practices is the code of silence. Lawyers are supposed to conduct their affairs in confidence, mob lawyers have to take this discretion to a much higher level. Many of the names and companies are actually fictitious; they are smokescreens to hide the real players. Compared to ordinary business law, this is a lot trickier

Sam is well paid, but knows he is earning every penny. Plus, with all of this information in the confines of his head, he is now every bit as deeply involved as the rest of the family. In fact, by necessity he is now a "made man."

Sam was far younger than the others around him and his original idea of working in the gray areas of the law are long since gone. He is a racketeer as defined by the government. It is like the old saw, "in for a penny, in for a pound." All of this secrecy and time commitment has made a huge dent in Sam's ability to have a permanent relationship with a woman. He has had many dates and short term romances with some fine and attractive women in New York, but the complexity of trying to fit someone permanently into his life always leads to an ultimate breakup.

As for his family back in Jersey, Sam gets to see them on holidays and special occasions. But even here, there is always a certain distance Sam feels as he can let no one, no matter how closely related, know his real career. It would be just too dangerous for them and him. So, Sam is conflicted. He has all of the material things he could ever want, but he is not progressing towards a possible family life, nor can he ever hope to change careers at this point. Sam knows it is the ultimate trade-off that every underworld figure has to make; he is no different.

Across town in his office sits Carlo Dellveccio, the mob boss for his family for the past fifteen years. We have all heard of the good old days, well Carlo feels this was certainly true for the five crime families that controlled New York. While there was the occasional bloodletting when new leaders or renegade soldiers of the various families attempted to expand their reach into another family's area, these transgressions were always dealt with and harmony again prevailed in New York. But now a new threat, that wasn't going to go away in a couple of weeks or even months, was rearing its ugly head.

The law was always a menace to the mob, but when you dealt with local authorities, you were up against one detective or at most a precinct Captain who was out to prove a point. However, when critical witnesses failed to show up for trials, there was little the local authorities could do. Sometimes it was necessary to pay off a couple of over vigilant cops or a meddling detective, but these were all manageable problems. The local authorities eventually lost interest as more pressing criminal matters were always at hand. Come the 1980s and new problems arrived.

This all went back to the early 1960s when Robert Kennedy became Attorney General in 1961 and began to investigate mob influence in legitimate businesses and unions. After his brother President John F. Kennedy was killed in 1963, Robert was out of the Attorney General's office and the pressure was off. Whether Robert and John Kennedy's assassinations had anything to do with the mob has never been proven, but it certainly did bode well for the families to have those two off of their backs forever. The other federal authority who could have been a threat to the crime families was J. Edgar Hoover's FBI. But Hoover, it has been alleged by some, had a long history of not wanting to get involved prosecuting organized crime in America. The reasons for this are not clear, but the results were good for the families across the nation.

Fast forward to the eighties and we have new problems. There is a law passed by Congress called RICO, an anti-racketeering statute that targeted the mob families. For the first time federal charges could now be brought for collusion to act together to commit crimes that were now punishable by federal instead of local statutes. Several Federal prosecutors in the States like Rudolph Giuliani in New York began to bring charges and get grand juries to indict, and later, in trials get convictions for mob members and their leaders. All of a sudden prominent family members had the light of the news media shone upon them, followed by aggressive prosecutions.

Carlo was one of the Dons who, while not himself indicted, had seen plenty of his peers make the 'perp' walk. When you add this to the development of much better forensic science especially DNA testing, it was getting easier for the authorities to get the evidence they needed for convictions. Thus the interest and need for the new 'firestop' project to be implemented.

Carlo had to at least slow down the advances made by the authorities on his turf. All of this for Carlo, this was a costly distraction to family business. He now has a couple of his Lieutenants under indictment and is being forced to pay for a costly legal defense. His lawyer, Sam, was more and more involved with these cases and Carlo had to spend countless hours in conference with him to guide the defense.

Worse, people who his soldiers dealt with, who paid ransom to the mob, were less fearful and more aggressive in their willingness to hold out. No, these were not the best of times for Carlo, but you have to play the hand that is dealt to you, and Carlo will soldier on.

A Call to Action

IT IS MONDAY morning following the organization's meeting and Sam has two new priorities to attend to. First, he contacts a criminal lawyer he has used in the past, one Saul Lassik. After a discussion of the Bruno Albino case particulars, Sam assigns the case to Saul. The two lawyers will stay in close contact, but for discretionary reasons, Sam will remain in the shadows on this one. Saul will be the Attorney of Record and do all of the courtroom work on the trial.

The second challenge is a bit more complex. For Sam it is completely out of his area of expertise. He now calls Mitch Gruber the 'go to guy' for finding out about how anything works in the business world. Mitch is asked to find out, how hard would it be to purchase and install a crematory in the New York metro area?

After two weeks, Mitch is sitting in Sam's office with a binder that includes full color literature on the latest retorts (the name for a cremation oven) available for cremation.

Mitch says to Sam, "So, you want to have a primer on cremation. It is really a quite interesting and dark enough subject that most people aren't going to want to know these details.

"First people have cremated the dead for as long as we have recorded history. The Hindus in India did and still do open fire cremations letting the ashes float down the Ganges River. They simply gather much kindling wood put the body on top and let it burn through the night. Besides not being good for tourism, it is quite toxic to the atmosphere. Fast forward to the eighteen hundreds and an Italian uses the technology already existent in gas commercial ovens like the kind used for baking. With a properly sized fire chamber, we can now accommodate a human body.

"The first modern crematory is born. This gives us a closed furnace usually fired by natural gas that is hotter, quicker, and much cleaner than open fire burnings. Fast forward another hundred years and the cremation manufacturers are now operating under even tighter pollution regulations and they respond with technology. Using computers and superchargers to blow high volumes of air onto the fire, temperatures are thereby increased substantially. The new retorts can get up to sixteen hundred to two thousand degrees Fahrenheit; this is the temperature that is needed to incinerate a body cleanly.

"With the EPA constantly decreasing the amount of pollutants allowed into the air, the companies respond by adding a second fire chamber above the main one housing the body. The purpose of this is to re-burn the gases from the first chamber in order to further purify the toxic residue in the escaping vapors. The final result is that you will see no black smoke or smell anything standing next to the air exhaust stack of a crematory. It is for all observable purposes just hot air coming out.

"The residue from the approximate two hour burn cycle are called cremains by the industry and ashes by everyone else. However they are really not ashes, they are bone fragments from the larger bones still left after the cremation. These two pounds or so of bone fragments are fed into a grinder called a processor and the outcome is a fine gravel. This uniform sized substance is then usually poured into an urn for further disposition.

"The final thing is that once this is done there can be no DNA or any other kind of known testing to determine who was in fact cremated. You couldn't even tell if it was man or woman, white or black.

The amount of ashes might give you some idea of the size of the person, but that would be very imprecise except that you may know it was an adult. If the remains are scattered or dumped in the sea there would soon be no trace of the ashes at all. And even if you recovered the ashes (cremains), they would be of no use for identification.

"This is a $50,000 to $75,000 piece of equipment and is a ten ton unit about the size of a car. It would fit into a one car space in a garage or any similar sized space. It is delivered on a truck in one piece, rolled into place and after the gas and three phase electricity connections are hooked up it is ready to go the same day."

All of this corresponded to what Victor had told Sam in Atlantic City during their meeting.

"This is the easy part," Mitch continues. "No one has their own private crematory. They are used to serve the public through funeral homes, cemeteries, and other service providers. Next, you need permits from the EPA and local authorities since it is an industrial furnace. In the New York metro area this could be a slow and arduous process as this would be one of the hardest areas in the country to quality with all of the additional local regulations. And this creates the third problem for you, how do you keep it secret. Once you apply for the permits everyone will know the name and address of the person/s who filed for the permits. Then, there are the constraints of the law for operating the retort. You need a signed cremation permit in every state for each body you run through the machine. This is why you can't just go to a legitimate crematory with a body for cremation. Where would the paperwork be? How long could a doctor and a funeral director keep forging these documents without getting caught? What professional would want to risk prosecution for aiding and abetting such a scheme?"

After spending the rest of the morning trying to twist and reformulate the subject to fit the organization's needs, Sam is pretty dejected. Sam feels, maybe this is why nobody has done this to his knowledge before, but there must be a way.

A couple of days after paying Mitch his $2,000 for the report, Sam is back in his office thinking about cremations. How do you justify the thing, if you don't have a funeral home or a cemetery? What professional would risk his career being involved in such a scheme of illegal cremations? It then occurs to Sam, what if you do have a funeral home in somebody else's name and it sits 100 miles from New York? An area much more secluded than Brooklyn, but less than three hours' drive away? What if that area was Northeast Pennsylvania and the operator might be desperate enough to engage in illegal activities? Sam knows he somehow has to get to Victor Kozol in Duryea, Pa.

But, how to approach someone about something illegal when to the best of your knowledge, this person is not involved in any illegal activities? How do you turn an honest guy? There has always been one answer to this problem, *money.* You offer more money than the person is making or has any hope of earning legitimately.

"It is even better to approach someone who is willing to gamble because he is already up against the wall financially. This formula has worked for the over one hundred years that the crime syndicates have operated in America. From federal judges, to shoe shine boys, the lure of easy money has allowed the underworld to operate freely in the legitimate world. Sam, for just a moment, reflects—this is exactly how I became involved. He will need to find out everything there is to know about Victor before he even attempts to contact him.

This takes Sam back to his Rolodex where a quick call to Serge Vlassic gets you a computer search on the personal information of anyone in America. It ain't cheap, but the info will have details you can't get on Google. Things like bank and credit card balances and payment records, FICA scores, outstanding loans, divorce decrees, convictions, you name it, if it exists Serge will find it.

'Firestop'

SAM HAS GOOD reason to be optimistic about his accidental
contact with Victor Kozol bearing fruit. If information is power
in this modern world, then Sam is powerful indeed. He now
has dossiers on: Victor; the Kozol Funeral Home; Vic's parents;
the boro of Duryea Pennsylvania; Pennsylvania Funeral and
Cremation Law; and more. Most important in this treasure trove
is the up-to-the-minute financial position and transactions of
Victor. He knows that Vic is getting close to insolvency and that
without some outside injection of cash, Vic will be out of business very soon. The only salvation other than Sam for Vic would
be if his parents intervened and gave him more financial aid. Sam
had to act first hoping to head off that exit for Vic.

So, Sam is ready to go to the next monthly meeting with a
formal request for *firestop*.

Sam is so confident that he strides into the meeting at Rosselli's
without any of this financial and personal information on Vic. He
knew that if he got permission none of that would be relevant.
He will use it to hook Vic, but the members of the organization
would only be bored by how he did it. Sam can only but think,
after this deal goes down successfully, Sam Gianetti will be the
man who beat police forensics at their own game. *Firestop* will
go down as a turning point in the organization winning against
law enforcement. The mob would now be able to operate with

impunity without fear of the reach of the long arm of the law. Best yet, Sam will be identified forever with this coup and be a rising star in the organization. But, like all good things, this project will require a lot of effort. However, Sam is thinking, no pain no gain.

Gathered around the same table at Rosselli's are the same faces Sam has sat across from for the last three years. At the end of the business agenda, Sam proposes that the organization authorize him to make contact with Victor Kozol for the purpose of fronting a crematory in his small upstate Pennsylvania funeral home. Sam recommends that Kozol Funeral Home will be the legal entity that owns and operates the retort. Victor himself will have to actually run the equipment and dispose of the ashes. He will be paid about twenty five times what a regular cremation pays for his services. The entire cost to install and set up the retort will be up to $100,000 and less if a lease for the retort can be worked out instead of purchasing it outright.

After that at $10,000 a pop for each cremation, the operation will be on a pay as you go system. Sam tells the group that we have to pay that much because Victor will not be able to stay afloat with his payments, as the entire cremation project makes no financial sense for Victor without the extraordinary help from the organization. This will also keep Victor from ever thinking he doesn't need our business. Carlo the Don has one important question, "How can we trust Kozol, an outsider? What if he says no to your scheme and goes to the cops?"

Sam tells Carlo, "I will be responsible for Kozol, if you greenlight the project."

He ends his comments with "No risk no reward."

After receiving an affirmative vote, Carlo reminds Sam whose idea this is, and who will be responsible if the project misfires. It is now 10:39 p.m. and the meeting is adjourned.

Victor and 'Firestop'

SAM NOW MUST turn his vague plan into concrete results. This will be the first big project that he is doing for the organization of his own initiation. Sam has to keep Victor from reaching out to other sources like his parents for help. He has to give him just enough so that Vic doesn't go under before Sam even has a chance to enlist him into the plan. First, Sam knows he just can't pitch Victor directly with this scheme or he risks his going to the police. He needs to ensnare Vic in a methodical and patient way. This has to be done correctly, Sam thinks, I get one chance to get this right. Since I don't know any other failing funeral directors, I need Victor.

Sam begins by calling an old associate from Brooklyn, Louis Premes. Lou is presently working as a pit boss at the blackjack tables at the Mountain Resort Casino in the Pocono Mountains in northeast Pennsylvania. Lou would rather be back in New York, but he fell behind in some heavy gambling debts with another family from Queens. Word was out on the streets of New York that it would be healthier if he wasn't there at this time. So wanting to stay healthy, Lou was breathing the fine clean air in the lovely Pocono Mountains of Pennsylvania.

Sam, through his contacts, obtained Lou's cell number and called in a favor. He needed Lou to assist a 'mark' he would bring into the casino to make some money. Lou could do this because it was only a scam for $5,000. This money Sam would reimburse so Lou could return it to the table. He then promised Lou $1,000 for helping.

The stage was now set to make the call inviting Victor to meet Sam in the Poconos for an old time's sake reunion. Victor took the call in his present state of depression without emotion. He really didn't feel like setting foot into another casino or for that matter wagering the kids outside for ice cream.

Sam says, "Vic, don't say no, I really enjoyed your company in Atlantic City and with the bonus I just got, I am buying dinner and drinks for old times' sake."

Victor does what he always does in these cases, first vacillates and then says yes. "Okay Sam, next Friday at 6:00 p.m. I'll meet you at Mountain Resort."

Sam drove west across Route 80 from New York that Friday, taking note how direct Route 80 was from the City to Pennsylvania. Two hours from the City and forty-five more minutes to Duryea, not bad he figures.

Sam, of course, already knew that Vic was at the end of his financial rope, and when he saw how depressed his old friend actually looked, he was sure with some smooth finessing, he could pull this off.

"How are you Vic," Sam calls out from the bar.

Vic smiles and tries to put on a happy face for the occasion.

"Let's get something to eat, I'm starved."

He guides Vic to Sherali's Steak House which is right behind the gambling tables on the main level. Two hours later, after much small talk about sports and other subjects, to keep Vic's mind off of his problems, they head for the casino floor. Sam steers Vic towards Lou's blackjack area. Upon arriving at a table, Sam pulls out of his pocket $100 worth of chips and hands them to Vic. "Here, use these they're lucky."

Victor isn't feeling lucky, but in ninety minutes he has turned the $100 into $5,000. For each time the dealer won a hand, Vic won three. Vic picks up the chips and says, "Look Sam let's at least split this, after all it was all your seed money to begin with."

"Not on your life, Vic, it's all yours, you made it happen," Sam responds.

"Oh by the way, Vic, now that I am this close, how about showing me your funeral home?"

"It's hardly worth you driving up to see my little place, Sam."

"Tomorrow, I have business in Scranton. How about I call you after lunch and update you on a time-frame I can be there?"

"Okay, Sam, if you want to be bored I can't stop you; come on over."

With that Vic and Sam take leave of each other.

Vic was feeling much better when Sam arrived the next afternoon. After all, he now had enough money to last out the month, and then he would worry about what comes next. Sam seemed to be very interested in the place considering he was a big 'city slicker' where they had funeral homes that did more funerals in a morning than Vic did in a couple months. Vic dutifully showed Sam everything. Sam seemed disappointed that even though this was a small town there was little space around the funeral home, which was just a large old home in the middle of town. In fact, there wasn't even a garage.

"Hey, Vic. Where do you keep the hearses and cars?"

"Well, when my father and grandfather were running it, they kept their cars in the old boro maintenance garage which grandpa bought sixty years ago from the boro."

"Still have it?" Sam asks.

"Sure, but it's down at the end of town."

"Can I see it?"

"I don't know why, all you will see is our old hearse and limousine that we haven't used for years. See, for the last several years we rent late model Cadillacs from a livery service in Scranton for each funeral. It just doesn't pay with our low volume to own the cars anymore."

"Hey, Vic, I love old cars, let's go see."

On a dead end street with no other homes or businesses sat a cinder block garage capable of holding ten cars. The property was surrounded by a chain link fence and the entire place was in disrepair from years of neglect. Victor has a hard time getting the key in the rusty lock, but finally the door swings open with a loud creak, like out of a scene from a horror movie. The look was eerie. Inside the dark, leaky, and musty building were two cars, a hearse, and a limousine from the 1970s sitting on a cracked concrete floor. In addition, some junk was strewn around, none of which seemed to be of much value.

Sam's eyes lit up. He is thinking, this place could hold several cremation retorts and it's big enough to pull a van in and close the door for total privacy while unloading. Better still, there is no one living nearby to see the traffic coming and going. In fact it's much more private than the funeral home back in the middle of Duryea. It looks like all of the pieces are coming together here. But, Sam knows he must wait for the proper time to spring his proposal. Victor has to once again run out of money, and this time Sam will be waiting. Victor and Sam shake hands and say their goodbyes and promise each other to stay in touch.

Throwing Out the Bait

SAM WAS IN a conflicted mood after leaving Victor and Duryea behind. Here was a young guy who never could get it together sinking in a financial morass mostly of his own making. Serge's reports have reinforced that none of this reflects on any criminality in Vic's life. He is what you would expect to find in small town America. Sam would rather be trying to do a deal with a shady operator in the Bronx than Mr. Clean in upstate Pennsylvania, but the shady operator in the Bronx didn't have a funeral home with all of the right pieces to the puzzle in place. So, Sam will have to work around Vic considering his family ties and solid background. He has promised too much to Carlo and the family to fail on this his first very own major project. Sam is determined not to fail.

Sam patiently lets another month go by carefully checking Vic's rapidly depleting checkbook balance which he views on-line from his office. The $5,000 that Sam engineered for Vic at the casino is now gone and it is time to act before Vic looks for other lifelines.

"Hello, Vic, I really needed to call you and see how you are getting along; because in all of our discussions I was so interested in what you did, that I never gave you details on how my specialty works. I operate primarily as a venture capitalist, Vic. My company invests in small businesses that we think have a good chance of turning a profit, even if they are not successful today."

"Well, you better look somewhere else, Sam, this place is rapidly going down the tubes after fifty years of continuous operation."

"See, Vic, this is where the optimist sees the glass half-full and my associates and I are constantly searching for new opportunities. It just so happens that I know this financial trends guru here in New York by the name of Saul. Just coincidentally, while having lunch with him, he is telling me about the great future all over the country for the cremation business. It is already heading for 40% of all deaths and set to climb even higher in the future."

"Yes, I know all of this from school, Sam, but I am too small and too broke to buy the equipment."

"Vic, that's where I come in. I make a financial model of how you will grow your business having the only cremation retort in your town. People will like dealing with you for their cremation needs because you have one stop shopping for them. You would be in the black in no time once set-up and running."

Sam knows in reality that at $400 a pop for doing a cremation wholesale for another funeral home and maybe $750 retail for one of his own clients, supporting a $50,000 piece of equipment would hardly be a good return on the investment for Vic considering the low volume of business he had. In fact, if you factor in the gas and electricity used, the operation would be deep in the red, unless you do hundreds of cases every year.

"Vic, why don't I have Saul, at no cost to you, do a proforma for your funeral home owning a crematory, and then we can talk about how you can finance it with some upfront loans from my company. Then you can pay it all back with profits from operations."

"Sure, okay, Sam. Call me when you have something, since not much is happening around here."

"Oh ,Vic, by the way, we will need your latest financials and tax information to make this work, can you send them to me right away?"

"Yes, I have some stuff here from my accountant, but I warn you it is not very impressive."

Sam already has all he needs on Vic's financials in front of him, but he can't let that cat out of the bag, so he responds, "Okay, Vic. You will be hearing from me soon."

Vic hangs up and his temporary euphoria is soon overtaken by the sodden state of his affairs. He probably will never be hearing from Sam again after he reads these financials, just as well anyway.

CHAPTER 16

Going for the Close

EVERY ASPIRING SALES trainee is taught first you engage the customer and answer all of their objections, and then you go for the close; you ask for their business. In one short week after their meeting, Sam is back on the phone to set the hook for the close.

"Hello, Vic, my good friends in accounting were able to get your proposal together in record time, it's what friends do for one another, right?"

Vic is stunned; he had no expectation to ever hear from Sam after his tour of his mundane funeral home and decrepit garage coupled with his poor financial statements.

"Sam, I still don't know, but if you think your idea would save my business, come on over and make your pitch."

In two days, Sam is sitting in Vic's cramped office in Duryea with pictures of the cremation retorts and many colorful spreadsheets all showing how much money the crematory would return after expenses.

Sam begins, "In fact, we don't even have to purchase the thing outright, we can take a five year lease on the equipment and only have to make monthly payments. Money you will generate from operating the retort. It may not be a fortune at first, but you will have a solid second cash flow to augment your funeral business. Your records show, you could really use this injection. It's a win,

win situation for both of us; I get a new client, even if a small one, and you get a chance to finally dig out from your financial problems."

Vic, like most people, likes the idea of gambling on a business venture with other people's money. "You mean you will front the entire venture to get me started including enough working capital, Sam?"

"Yes, Vic, we know this project doesn't get off the ground unless venture capital comes to the rescue. No regular bank would ever front this deal without money up front from you, Vic."

"In that case, hand me the contracts and show me where to sign."

"Okay, Vic, I have it all drawn up, first is the retort lease application for $1,200 per month for five years, and second is the loan documents for the $25,000, we think you will need to remodel the garage and get the retort up and running, plus a little left over for working capital. We even got you all of the applications for the federal, state, and local approvals you will need for installing a crematory. You just need to sign, couldn't be easier. See how simple getting into business with me is; now, let's go to that great Italian restaurant you were telling me about in Old Forge, I'm buying."

Onward, Upward, & Downward

VICTOR HAS HIS check for $25,000 and in two short weeks everything is signed and sealed. In another month he gets his approvals from the local authorities to install and operate the crematory retort. Finally, Vic has something to live for. He is going to Chicago for three days to attend a school for operating his new retort. He is also hiring contractors to renovate and repair the old garage so that it can accommodate the new retort and look more presentable. In another month the retort is in and operating. Victor puts out advertisements in the local papers and church bulletins announcing his new venture, "Duryea's own crematory." The second day he gets his first client family from his own funeral home, and is really feeling great about the future.

Like so many business ventures, that are poorly or only half thought out, the flaws in the crematory model were always there, but Vic wasn't in any mood to look too hard for them. First, many of the townspeople have already written Vic off as a foul ball, not to be considered as their funeral director. Once you lose a client family to another funeral director, as happened with the Makovsky's, the rest of the extended family will also start going to your competitor. The only other place you can get cremation business is from your competitors or other out-of-town funeral directors.

Here, if Vic would have not been so euphoric about Sam's great opportunity he could have made a couple of phone calls and found out the stark truth. Competitors rarely will use a crematory in the same town operated by another funeral director. They don't want the other funeral director to see the amount of cremations they are doing and the type of merchandise they are selling for their cremations. They will gladly schlepp their bodies up to Scranton rather than do business with a competitor. Bottom line, there was no outside business for Vic from the local funeral directors in his hometown.

After two months in operation Vic has used his new retort all of two times for his own client families. While he grossed $1200.00 for his work, he has already paid out $2,400 in lease payments for the past two months. Added to this are the electric and natural gas bills of a couple of hundred dollars for the retort.

When you carry this loss forward to his losses on the funeral home side, where he is only doing about half the business of his father, Vic is sinking even faster with the crematory. He has $5,000 left from the original $25,000 startup money, but he owes both his father rent, and the real estate taxes on the properties.

Vic sits down and wonders after this initial period, where did I go wrong? Why are the pro forma projections not even near being met on the income side? The only thing he could think of was to appeal to the one guy who got him into all of this Sam, he would have an answer.

"Sam, is that you? It's your buddy, Vic. I need to talk to you."

"Anything for an old friend and client, what's bothering you, Vic?"

"I think I may need more working capital to get the crematory going. Maybe another $20,000 would see me through until the crematory starts pulling its own weight."

"Well, Vic, I didn't expect this news, this is most disappointing and a serious setback in our relationship."

Chapter 17

"Okay, then just $5,000 to hold me over, Sam."

"Look, Vic, you don't seem to have this situation under control and even your cash needs are wildly off the mark, I think you should come to my office in New York so that we could hammer out an agreement."

"Okay, Sam, I can be there tomorrow, nothing to do around here, how about 11:00 a.m.?"

Sam couldn't have been more delighted, Vic is running out of cash about a week before Sam projected it to happen. Sam will certainly be ready with a hammer to bludgeon out a deal with Victor when he arrives tomorrow.

The Hammer

VIC STARTS OUT early the next morning. It's a beautiful fall day. The leaves are just beginning to turn and as he approaches the granite cliffs of the Delaware Water Gap heading east into New Jersey on Route 80, the scenery is even more magnificent. There are golds, reds, and yellow all blending into what could be a beautiful painting. But, Vic is not paying much attention to nature around him.

For the first time he has a certain foreboding about the upcoming meeting in Brooklyn. He knows he was in a real mess on his own accord, but listening to Sam and his crematory advice only seems to have made it worse. Well, Sam got me into this part of my problems, so I will let him get me out. Just a little more working capital would smooth everything over.

At 11:10 a.m. Vic walks into Sam's sumptuous offices. The building is an old brick five story affair that could be over one hundred years old. But once inside, things were very different. The lobby, halls and elevators are sleek stainless steel trimmed with wood accents. The floors are marble and silver chandeliers dot the ceilings. Expensively dressed fine looking ladies with their high heels clicking on the Italian marble saunter through the halls with the other visitors. Victor thought, "These must be the secretaries and paralegals." At any rate he was duly impressed.

Stepping off the elevator at the fifth floor, the decor was even more luxurious with Sam's office suite in the north corner of the building. Upon entering, a receptionist who could be considered a "ten" greeted Vic and said Sam would be out in a minute. The office suite is done in cherry wood with dark green accents on the walls and a woolen Berber carpet graces the floor. Vic thought, "What a far cry from his lawyer Steve Lamont's spartan quarters back in Duryea. Sam is no $100 an hour lawyer like Steve."

"Victor my friend, it's so good to see you in New York." He guides Vic into his palatial corner office with the great view of the Brooklyn Bridge.

Sam gestures for Vic to take a leather arm chair in front of his teak, gold inlaid desk, and then takes his place facing Vic.

"This is like out of the movies, Sam."

"I guess I don't appreciate it as much as I see it every day; by the way how was the trip?"

"I enjoyed the ride and traffic was light, I can't get over your beautiful digs here, but all of that being said, I can't feel good about my position as to why I'm here."

"Perhaps we can solve some of your pressing problems today then go out and celebrate."

"I appreciate the thought, Sam, but after my episode earlier in the year down in Bucks County, I won't be doing any drinking today."

"Okay, but we can still do some great food later."

Vic opens the conversation and gets right to the point. "Look Sam, I missed the monthly payment for the retort lease, and I don't have the $3,000 I own my father this month. That's why I asked for a little more cash up front."

"I don't want to make a bad situation worse, Vic, but if you read page sixteen in your loan documents, you owe a payment to my associates on the $25,000 they loaned you. With the five year amortization and 15% APR interest, you owe another $800 for your start-up loan times two months, that's another $1,600 you need to come up with."

"Wow, I forgot about that, I guess that makes bankruptcy inevitable for me."

"Not so fast Vic, bankruptcy is an escape for some, but might not work in your case."

"What do you mean by that, I read about people declaring chapter 11 or whatever you lawyers call it every day."

"Look, Vic, here are the facts; the retort lease was cosigned by my venture capitalist associates. When you add that $50,000 they will be liable for if the retort lease is terminated prematurely, they are on the hook for $75,000."

"Oh shit, I'll never get that much money together in one place to ever pay it back."

"Right, and bankruptcy won't solve it for you because you don't own any of the real estate in Duryea."

"There is very little my associates could get back in a bankruptcy proceeding."

"Okay, so what else is there, you seemed to have closed the door on the only option people have in my situation."

"Well here is where it gets a little . . . shall we say dicey, Vic, see my friends here in the City are having a problem that you are the only one they can turn to for help. If you would help them out, they would not only forgive all of the debt you owe them, but they would reward you generously for your services."

Vic doesn't know what is coming next, but he is smart enough to know it will not be something he ever thought of while driving down here. He starts to squirm in his chair and for the first time feels really uncomfortable. Vic regains his composure and retorts, "What do they need done by me in Pennsylvania that they can't get done right here in New York?"

"They need a sort of specialized disposal service, Vic."

"A disposal service?"

"Yes, they need your crematory retort to make some things go away for them."

"Again, I am at a loss why can't they get the same services without all of the hauling expense to Pennsylvania right here in New York?"

"Victor, I'm afraid I just have to be direct here; they need a few dead bodies to disappear every year."

"What? Are you crazy man? You mean cremate some bodies which are evidence that the mafia or underworld wants to dispose of?"

"You make it sound so sinister Vic; look, there are no cameras or counters on your retort. When you push the buttons some gas and electricity gets used but there is no record of that cycle anywhere. There is no trace except for the two pounds or so of remains that the operation ever took place. Poof, the body and all evidence of it disappear forever."

"No way man, I need a cremation permit from some state agency for each cremation that I perform, that gives me legal permission to do it."

"See, Vic, you said it yourself, a small eight by eleven inch piece of paper is all that is coming between you and the solution to all of your problems."

"Yah, but that little piece of paper means breaking the law and jail time for me the operator."

"Getting caught would be highly unlikely, Vic. But, the problem for me is in your case I can't talk these investors into anything else. They don't need anything else and you don't have anything to give them anyway; they just need a few already dead bodies to disappear, Vic. You don't have to know who they are or where they came from or anything about them. You simply push the buttons, drop the remains in the Lackawanna River and get paid."

"How much would they pay me for a criminal act like that?"

"My friends have informed me that they would forgive all of the start-up costs and pay you $10,000 a case going forward."

"$10,000 a case, are you kidding me man?"

"My associates don't kid about business decisions of this gravity, Vic."

"Well, Sam, I have to go home and sleep on it, this is a momentous decision for me; this is far outside of anything I ever dreamed about in my entire life."

"Vic, I wish there was the luxury of time for you, but I need an answer now."

"Well then, I guess it's going to have to be a no, Sam. But thanks for all of the help."

"No, Vic, we can't end it just like that, it would be easy for you, but not for me to face my associates, so I propose we do the 'Ben Franklin' close on this matter. That is we take a piece of paper," Sam tears off a sheet from a notepad and writes on the top reasons for and against, and draws a line down the center.

"See, we will now list all of the reasons for and against my proposal, whichever side comes out with the best reasons, is the side you do, okay?"

"Yah, on one side I get money until I go to jail."

"No, Vic, on one side you remain a trusted businessman keeping up with all of his obligations in the community. Plus you are living a lifestyle far better than you enjoy now."

"On the other side," Sam points to the pad's right side, "You are a disgraced former funeral director with a target on his and his families back."

"What target, Sam?"

"Vic, I told you your insolvency leaves my associates out $75,000 with no place to collect it except from you personally or maybe your parents."

"No way man; you can't threaten my parents, they have nothing to do with any of this." I'm just saying, Vic, how else can these investors get their money back?"

"Wow, I may need police protection and soon."

"Wait, Vic, who are you going to be protected from? There are no notes or threats recorded on your life, or people waiting outside your door to get you. Do you really think the police are going to protect you forever on some flimsy hearsay evidence? The answer is that even in Duryea, they aren't going to devote two of their four man police force watching you. I mean, Vic, you are in no immediate danger, but you can never tell a month or even a year down the road what could happen."

"Geez, I can't believe I am having this conversation with you, Sam."

"Vic, if it was just me, I would let bygones be bygones, I would say, the guy tried his best let's forget about it."

"What friends you have, Sam, I am just realizing who you really represent."

"Vic, I guess we are all disappointed at how this worked out, but you have to make a decision here. Go home and call me by the end of the week as to where you stand. Longer than that, and I just may not be able to control things at this end."

"Sam, I'll take a rain-check on dinner, I'm not hungry right now, but you will hear from me, I promise." Vic leaves Sam's office with a new emotion; fear. This one seems to top the ones of lethargy and despondency.

Fight or Flight

VIC IS BACK on Route 80, heading west towards
Pennsylvania. As you approach the Delaware Water Gap from
this direction the terrain becomes very rugged with towering
rock cliffs that had to be blasted through to make the openings
for the highway. As he sullenly and robotically guides his car
along over the pavement, Vic's mind races on to alternative
courses of action. He sees the one hundred foot rock ledge fifty
feet to his right. He thinks, 'what if I just let the car drift into the
granite, it would all be over in a flash. But then an even scarier
scene enters his muddled brain. He is not dead, but in an ICU
unit of a local hospital after the crash. Hovering over him lying
helplessly with all kinds of restraints on is a dark shadowy figure
standing on the oxygen line hooked to Vic's nose. There is no
escape from Sam's organization. Vic is choking and gasping for
air and ready to black out when reality returns.

With his mind wandering wildly, he now goes back to the first
scene where he is dead underneath the wreckage of his car after
hitting the rock ledge. However, now the same dark figure is
hovering over his sleeping parents in Florida with a knife. Again
Vic feels if they can't recover the money from him they will move
to the next closest members of his family. What about his sister,
could they track her and her family down? By the time Vic is
safely back in Duryea he is mentally and physically exhausted

from the day's happenings and all those weird thoughts he was entertaining on the road.

The next morning Vic gets up at 11:00 a.m. and still feels exhausted. It takes him but a minute to relive the events of yesterday and all of his other problems putting him back into a horrible mood. Vic gets dressed and heads for the local coffee shop. Here at the counter he spies an old friend of his father, Charley Heckman. Charley was chief of police here in Duryea for thirty years until his retirement some ten years ago. Vic moves over closer to Charley to initiate a conversation.

"Charley, how are you, my father often asks about you?"

"Oh it's Vic, very good after all who wants to hear old people complain anyway?"

"Charley, let me pose a hypothetical question to you. If a local citizen is being threatened by someone from out of the area, and they wanted to get some protection, how would they go about it?"

"I hope this isn't about you or your family, Vic."

"No, no, but I had a widow that I was arranging a funeral for and her daughter was in this predicament up in Eynon."

"Well, Vic, she can go to the local police up there, but she is going to need some particulars for them to even look into it."

"What kind of particulars, Charlie?"

"The police will need names, places, dates, and a description of the incident, even with all of that, unless a crime has already been committed, they can't do a whole lot. There are just not the resources anywhere to station guards around her daughter and her home. There would have to be some type of local threat occurring that they could respond to, otherwise they are chasing ghosts."

"Ghosts, maybe that's what my client's daughter is chasing after all, well thanks, Charley, for the info, if she calls back, I can tell her what you told me."

"So, Sam is exactly right," thought Vic. *What police department: local, state or federal can hang around waiting for something to happen. They will certainly investigate if Vic is found dead in his home or on the street, but by then the horse has sort of left the proverbial barn.* This idea of coming clean to the police is receding further and further into the background.

The next thought of ignoring Sam in New York was entertained as in normal times this would be Vic's default position on any crisis; do nothing. But even Vic knows that this time he is in too deep to just ignore the problem. What about just leaving everything behind and starting a new life somewhere, anywhere else? This initially sounds like a good plan. You fill the car with gas, throw some clothes in the trunk and vamoose.

But, there is a reality check with this idea also. First, Vic is almost out of funds in the bank and his credit cards are almost completely maxed out. If he just gets a couple hundred miles away and runs out of money, who do you turn to? If you start working somewhere under your own name, you are exposed to being found. This would be especially true after Vic's family and friends file police reports that something suspicious happened to him, as he is inexplicably gone. There would be locater requests sent out all over the country by the local authorities looking for him.

Finally, if he changed his identity, he would need resources to get that accomplished. Probably the only employer who wouldn't want to see valid ID for a job would be a migrant farm labor contractor. So, running is not what it initially seems and it would likely be just temporary. Worse, the mob could locate him out of town first and that would be curtains. Just when Vic couldn't be any more walled in by his circumstances the second blow falls.

The next day, Vic's father unexpectedly called at 10:00 a.m. arousing Vic from a deep sleep. "Vic, as you already know the check for this month's rent never appeared, and I am damned tired of pulling teeth to get what is owed to me. It should come as no surprise to me, Vic, because more than a couple of friends have called us from Duryea telling us how badly things were going up there with the funeral home. It is time for tough love, Vic. I am issuing you an ultimatum, if I don't see the money in two days, I will get on a plane and evict you from the premises. Then, I will sell what is left of the business and the property.

By the way, they tell me you now have a crematory in the garage. I guess I now know where my rent money is, in some fool project of yours. Well the days of playing with my money are over, Vic. I hope this brings you to your senses; know that I will wait until the end of the week, two more days, that's it, so long." Click.

"Just as well he hung up on me, as I have no money or answers for him that he is going to like," thought Vic.

Now Vic has heat coming from two stereo channels New York and Florida at the same time. Sam didn't know how perfect the timing of Vic's father was for his purposes, but it was the final straw that forced Vic into action.

"Sam, it's me, Vic. Look, maybe I was a little hasty about walking out on you last week."

"Vic, you were under stress and I fully understand how startled you were by my proposal. I just hope that these couple of days gave you time to come to the right decision."

"Oh it has, Sam, but before we can begin with your deal, I will need a quick $10,000 advance to keep going. Otherwise there won't be a business left here for your associates to make use of."

"Vic, you will have the $10,000 wired to your account today, as far as proceeding on the other matter, I will be in touch later."

"Thanks, Sam, I know this will work out for the both of us."

Sam puts the phone in its cradle and breathes a sigh of relief. All of the planning and time spent is going to finally pay off. Sam will be the star of the next meeting with the organization.

Under the Spell of the Mob

AFTER TWO WEEKS, Vic was feeling a lot better with his financial reprieve which allowed things to calm down in Duryea. But, when you make a pact with the devil it is certain that he will be back to collect his part of the bargain. A simple ring of the phone was about to change Vic's life forever.

"Hello, Vic, it's me, Sam, seems like it is time for you to honor your part of our deal."

"Okay, Sam, I was wondering when you would be calling me. What can I help with?"

"First, you need to come back to New York and we'll give you the necessary instructions for the mission."

"When, Sam?"

"How about tomorrow afternoon, Vic"

A lump rose in Vic's throat, but he knew there is no turning back now,

"I'll be there tomorrow at 2:00 pm, Sam."

"Okay, see you then."

Vic is sitting in Sam's conference room, an even more exotic room than his office. Inlaid marble floors, a huge mahogany conference table, and modern paintings adorn the walls. Not to mention the view of the bridge. With Sam is a smaller older rough-around-the-edges kinda guy who looks like he is stuffed into his suit. Sam introduces Vinnie as the go between for Vic in this operation. Vinnie does not disappoint in his portrayal of a TV type mob character complete with a Brooklyn accent.

"Pleezed ta meet witcha, Vic," says Vinnie.

"Same here, Vinnie," Vic replies finding these types of characters actually exist in real life incredible.

"Okay, Sam says, now that the formalities are over, we talk about procedures going forward. First, Vic, you will always have your cell with you. A black van with a "package" will depart New York whenever there is a need. Vinnie will call you at this time to alert you. When the van reaches Route 81 near Scranton which should take little over two hours, you will get a call with the code word "Rubik." If everything is alright at your end, you will answer "Cube." You don't have to say another word. You will then go to the garage, leave the lights off and open the overhead door. When the van enters, you will immediately close the door. Vinnie, the driver, will help you unload the *package* and place it into the retort. He will leave you with an envelope containing $10,000 at this time. Vic is to ask no questions of Vinnie who will then leave Vic alone.

"Vic, you are under no circumstances to look into or ever open the *package* but simply start the cremation process and wait the two hours for the cycle to complete, after the retort cools you are to gather up the remains and dump them into the nearby Lackawanna River. Further, involve no one else to help you. It goes without saying that 'loose lips sink ships' and the first one to sink will be yours if you ever divulge a word of this to anyone.

"When the entire mission is completed you are to dial 201-666-7887 and leave the code word "fire stopped" on the answering machine. With that, the mission is over until you hear from Vinnie again. Is that clear, Vic? Now, repeat all of this back to me."

Vic complies and again is feeling shaky as he is this close to an evil he only thought existed in TV shows. "One final thing, Vic, this is not going to be an everyday or even once a week thing, but when we do call, you had better be there. Because the only way this thing stays together is that there be no down time between any of these steps. We can't have vans with dead bodies circling around waiting to make their drop, kabish, Vic?"

"Sam, I'll do my part, not to worry."

Vic returned home knowing the real show will begin shortly; this was just the dress rehearsal. The only reason he wants the phone to ring is that he is almost through the $10,000 that Sam wired him. He will soon need another cash injection to survive. "The compromises we make to stay alive," thought Vic.

Charley Jones

CHARLEY JONES WAS born in Bayonne, New Jersey, just across the Hudson from New York. After high school he migrated to Brooklyn in search of better opportunities. Charley wasn't one for books at school or any strict discipline at work. Therefore, he was always a short timer with many different low skilled jobs clogging up his resume. He would go through jobs in a month or two. He was: a driver, kitchen helper, dock worker, and janitor and many other titles in his career. He is now thirty-nine and finally found a home with the syndicate as a low level runner and collector. While not a great fighter, at six feet and two hundred pounds he exuded some authority on the street.

Charley has a route which has him meeting gambling clients for his boss Joey Torchia, who is a Lieutenant for the DellVeccio family. Charley either picks up the bets or delivers the winnings in his area. Contacts are made by cell phone and meetings can be anywhere from a subway station to a local bar. Charley then meets Joey usually once or twice a week depending on business at Joey's favorite watering hole The Blue Dragon. In the back room they settle up and Charley is usually given $300 to $500 in cash for his work.

All was going well for Charley as he was making more money than his low level dead end jobs of the past. Charley on his way to making some heavy payoffs to high roller gambling customers of Joey is sometimes carrying over $10,000 cash in winnings. He would like to be one of those winners, but he has no seed money to make the bets. So, he comes up with a plan to get some folding money to make some bets on horses and sporting events.

Charley has a friend in his apartment building, Jack, who as a longshoreman is as strong and tough of a guy as you will find in this neighborhood of Brooklyn near the docks. Charley meets up with Jack at their favorite bar, Orgo's. He approaches Jack at the bar and casually says, "I will give you $100.00 if you give me a non-bone breaking working over some night."

Jack looks at Charley and says, "Why do you want this"?

"It's better you don't know, Jack."

They finish their beers and leave with Jack thinking, Charley had a few too many tonight. But the next week, Charley finds Jack once again at Orgo's and says, "It's time for me to get roughed up."

The reason he is asking Jack now is that Charley has just come from meeting Joe Torchia and is carrying $28,000 cash, the largest amount he ever carried. All of this was to be delivered to five different winners that night.

After buying enough beers for Jack, Jack agrees to do this fool's errand in the back alley behind the bar. The beating results in Charley losing a tooth, getting two black eyes and plenty of other facial and body bruises. Charley is already regretting what he thought was an 'easy' way to make money. Already through the bad part, he figures he has to go through with the scheme. He first goes to a nearby cemetery, and puts the $28,000 in a coffee can and buries it under a large oak tree, so that is would be easy to recover.

Next he searches out Joey while he is still looking his worst. "Joey, I don't know how this happened, but I got jumped up in Bay Ridge Parkway on the way to making my first payoff. I can't believe it but these guys got my 'er your cash."

Joey has seen all of this before, but has to be sure if Charley is playing him or if he's legit. Joey says, "Charley, get in my car and the two of us will think this through."

"Sure, Joey, anything to help get your money back."

While Charley is walking towards Joey's Cadillac, Joey is making a cell call. Joey then drives Charley around making some stops and inquiries along the way. The pair ends up at an abandoned house in one of the bad parts of Brooklyn. Joey leads Charley up the steps and into the darkened house. Charley is immediately grabbed by two of Joey's enforcers thrown in a chair where his arms and legs are tightly secured with plastic ties.

"What's this? It's not my fault that the money is gone, we should all be outside looking for the bad guys."

"That is what we are here to find out, Charley, just who are the bad guys." Joey leads off with "Now tell me again just where and when did this unpleasant incident occur?"

"I told you all I know, it happened so fast."

Wham! Charley takes the first blow of a second and much worse beating to come. After a couple of minutes of pummeling over his face and body by the two enforcers, Charley is limp in the chair.

"Shall we continue?" asks Joey.

"No, please, I don't know any more than I already told you."

Thump, he is hit again hard in the solar plexus, and is now with good reason more afraid than he has ever been before. Charley thinks fast to avoid the next round he knows is surely coming. "Look, I think one of the guys was this Jack, big dock-worker who hangs around Orzos on Third Avenue. For the other two I can't be sure, it happened too fast for me to get a good look at them."

"Well I'll tell you what, Charley, we are going to pay a little visit to Jack and get our money back."

"Sure, Joey, that's the quickest way to end all of this."

The three mobsters leave Joey soaked in blood and urine and go out to find Jack. After some questioning of bar patrons and the owner of Orzos, they get Jack's address and go to his apartment.

As soon as Jack answers his doorbell, he is pushed inside by the two thugs, "What's this, I don't know you guys."

Joey emerges behind the two goons. "No, but you know where our $28,000 is and according to Charley Jones, you were one of the perps."

"I know nothing."

With that Joey pulls out his Smith & Wesson snub nose thirty eight and points it at Jack's temple while the other two thugs are restraining him.

"Now one time and one time only, what happened between you and Charley and where's my $28K?"

"Look, honest guys you have no fight with me, Charley came and gave me a hundred bucks to be worked over just enough so that he would look bad. He never said why, but I got my hundred and I left, that's all I know. I should have figured Charley was up to something, but I was half in the bag from too many beers to care. He never told me nothing, I swear."

"Let him go guys," Joey says as he holsters his gun, "I think I know where the problem is."

"Look, Jack, no hard feelings, here's another hundred for your troubles," Joey says as he stuffs the "C" note into Jack's shirt pocket. "Oh, and by the way, we were never here."

"Thanks guys, glad to have never known ya." With that Joey and his two enforcers head back to the abandoned house where they left Charley.

"Is it alright Joey, did Jack admit to beating me up?"

"Yes, Charley, as a matter of fact he did, but there is still a little matter of the missing money. He doesn't have it."

"Oh, see one of the other shorter guys must have taken it."

With that Joey gives Charley a backhand across the face the force of which turns the chair on its side ending with a huge crash that sends Charley to the floor with the chair on top of him. He is screaming with pain.

Joey says, "Now here's what's going to happen. We are going for a little ride wherever you say to go and at the end of this drive you are going to produce the money, Kabish?"

Charley knows there are no more evasions he can use and he can't stand the pain of more beatings, so he directs the driver to St. Gabriel's Cemetery. After being dragged into the cemetery, he points to a large oak tree. "Go get it, Joey bellows."

With that Charley limps to the spot, falls to his knees and starts digging with his hands, soon unearthing the coffee can.

"Now wasn't that easy, Charley?"

"Sure, Joey, I must have lost my mind for a brief moment, but I was going to deliver the money tomorrow."

"Throw this piece of shit in the trunk and head for the docks."

Charley is so scared he stops feeling the pain from his multiple beatings, and he knows better than to make any noise in the trunk. After arriving at a darkened warehouse, the electric roll up door rises and slowly closes behind Joey's Cadillac as they drive into the cavernous empty space. Joey gets through to Carlo for permission to off Charley. He gets the green light plus some new instructions for disposing of the body.

They pull Charley from the trunk and frog march him to the far windowless wall. Without any further exchanges, Joey pulls out his pistol and puts two slugs in Charley's head. In the old days it would be up to the executioner to come up with a way of disposing of the body, but now a new order has come out from Carlo. A call is made to Vinnie, the contact man for the new disposal service. In thirty minutes Vinnie is in the warehouse with his black suburban. He reaches in and pulls out a vinyl disaster pouch. This is a pouch with six handles and a full length zipper made to hold one body. It is used primarily for mass casualty situations like airplane crashes. The others help Vinnie, place Joey's body in the pouch and zip it up. After the suburban is loaded, the pouch is covered with some eight-foot long 2 x 4s. Vinnie makes his first historic call to Victor in Duryea. Charley after all needs a proper disposal.

By 9:00 p.m. Vinnie is helping Vic load the pouch into the retort. He hands Vic his envelope and promptly leaves to go back to New York. By midnight the cremation is finished and the retort has been cleaned out and a short trip to the Main Street Bridge sees the remains slowly drifting down to the roaring river below. Vic certainly didn't like the disposal part, but the $10,000 was the easiest money he ever made. He didn't fall asleep for the longest time that night. But by the next morning it was just like a dream from the past.

CHAPTER 22

Euphoria at Rosselli's

BACK IN NEW York, the weekly dinner meeting of Carlo's family has good reason for celebrating. After years of frustration with prosecutions and convictions from DNA and other evidence bedeviling the family, finally there is something good to report. The first disposal by cremation has occurred and it is a success. While the subject of this project one Charley Jones was a really minor player, it is a fact that this new crematory works and that bodes well for the future. The report of Sam Giannetti makes him the star of the show tonight. For a minimum expenditure of less than $50,000 the family has a permanently installed facility to use into the foreseeable future. Its location, one hundred miles from New York, is far enough away from any local jurisdictions, that it should be next to impossible to connect Duryea, Pennsylvania with Brooklyn.

The only weak link would be the operator in Pennsylvania, and Sam assures his colleagues that Victor is as solidly committed to this as if he were part of our family. That remark is probably a stretch, given the instability of Victor's personality. The same weaknesses that brought Victor aboard, could work against the family if pressure is ever exerted on Victor by any law enforcement authorities. Victor has been turned once, maybe he could be turned again and render state's evidence. This is a question that no one is asking on this Friday night.

The other members of the group of twelve are only looking at the subject as a typical legit business venture they do all the time. They buy into a business; once they own it the operations will now be skewed towards the new owners. It was much like buying the Ajax garbage disposal company last month. This was the last independent hauler in Brooklyn who was undercutting the mob's prices. Presto, the Ajax prices are now higher than the mob's other haulers. And no one can say anything, because Sam has the deed for the Ajax Corporation in his safe.

Carlo instructs the group that after getting approval from him for a hit, Vinnie is to be contacted immediately after the hit and the transfer of the body to him will happen at one of the dock warehouses that are secure. This policy will be effective until further notice. Also, the members can put out the word to their lieutenants that we can now become more aggressive in handling transgressors. Just like with Charley Jones, we don't have to only target problems at the higher end we can tighten up the ranks down to the runners and bag men. All agree this could put the family back to the position of strength they enjoyed in the good old days, when they could whack most anyone with impunity and walk away.

Yes, it is a new day and Carlo orders the wine steward to break out a couple bottles of the finest French Champagne for the celebration. However, this is a celebration that must stay cloistered within the four walls of this room; this was the case with most of the activities of Carlo's family.

Jack Cardigan

IT HAS OFTEN been a joke among those in the know that the mob needs enforcers who turn to violence for collections because they can't sue for payment in a court of law. Yes, the verbal contract you make with your bookie would never see the light of day in any American court. There is no redress for an illegal action. So, crime families have to employ their own enforcers to bring in outstanding debts. Sometimes special members do nothing but enforce. These are the guys who are the bone breakers and possibly even executioners. But, like all collection agencies, the mob will first resort to the regular bag men and runners whom the bets were placed with in the first place.

Jack Cardigan has been gambling with his Dellveccio "bag-man" Luigi, for the last several years. Jack having no family or other responsibilities spent his extra money winning and losing each week. Jack thoroughly enjoyed himself watching the ponies run, and professional sports bets. But when Jack loses his job as a maintenance man on Wall Street, his spending and living money dries up quickly.

While he is looking for new employment, he rationalizes that only through placing heavier bets can he come up with the cash he will need to sustain himself. No gambler ever looks at his past track record to see if this theory really justifies putting in larger wagers. The thrill of the action is too great to consider this. Jack empties his savings of $6,000 and places heavy bets on a couple of games and five ponies in various races for the week. He wins one race and one game, but the losses take out half of his starting capital.

He then appeals to his man Luigi, to get him some credit from the house for next week's gambling. Luigi tells him he is good for $10K on the cuff. A grateful Jack now bets another $5K on ponies and games. He loses $3K when the week's tally is in. He carries on like this for two more weeks with the result he is wiped out. He now lost his $5K of savings and another $10K loan from the organization . . .

Jack is now spending more time at Bozos, his favorite local bar drowning his sorrows and watching games and races he can no longer bet on. Three weeks later on a Wednesday night he is returning to his apartment late when he is startled to hear a familiar voice behind him. Turning around he sees Luigi quickly closing the distance and coming up alongside of him.

"Watsamatta, Jack, you no longer talk to Luigi? Well, Jack, right now you and me gotta talk. See da boss is asking me for da $10K plus the $1K interest you owe us fur last month, he tinks maybe you don't like us anymore and took your business elsewhere."

"No, no, Luigi, I've been out of work for a couple weeks, I don't have the dough right now, but I'm working on something, and then I can get straight with you guys again."

"No, Jack, now you listen, dat is not a date or a place when da dough is coming for repayment. No bank or loan company would accept dat explanation, why shuz I?"

"Well, Luigi when you strip away all of the talk here, I got no job, assets, or other income to pay you back with. You might even compare me with a very large turnip, if you squeeze it nothing comes out."

"See, Jack, dat is where your tingin ain't holdin no water, you ain't no turnip, and if you are squeezed sometin will come out, and it won't be good for your long term healt, kabish? Please don't insult me with dis attitude, I am only trying ta do what is best fur your future."

"Are you threatening me, Luigi?"

"You can call it what you like, but da next guy ta see you may not be like me, and he won't have my patience wit dis very important matter. I tink you come up with some money and call me in da next couple of days so dat you and me can work dis out like gentlemen."

"I'll try, Luigi, but threatening me isn't going to get your money back."

Jack is plenty scared, but he is hoping that $10K isn't enough to bring the real bone breaking enforcers down on him. Three days later he calls Luigi and lies, "Luigi, I got a lead on a restaurant job downtown, but it will take time to get the money together from working there. Right now I have zero to give you"

"Alright Jack have it your way, bye."

After another week Jack is home one night really worried about still no job and the gambling debt. But he can do nothing, because he is trapped in a situation he has no control over. The door buzzer sounds and Jack hollers "Who is it?"

"UPS," the voice from the other side of the door responds.

Jack doesn't think he ordered anything, but he instinctively opens the door. With that all hell breaks loose, as two goons tumble into his living room and force Jack down into his TV chair.

"Luigi sends his regards," the larger of the two says as he pounds Jack in the stomach with a clenched fist.

"Ugh," Jack cries out.

"We are going to ask you just once nicely, duh you have da money fur us?"

Jack shakes his head, but the motion is stopped by a volley of fists as he gets pummeled in the face by the second goon. He grunts in pain, but the fists keep flying, until Jack is bloodied and slumped over limp and near passed out in his chair.

"Enough, Enrico," says the first goon, "Listen real careful, Jack, dis ain't nutin compared to what happens if we don't hear from you wit da money next week."

With that they leave as quickly as they entered. Jack is panting, sweating, and might have soiled himself after the last horrible five minutes. He is almost immobilized and his face is really starting to throb. Who to call, and what to say? Jack spends the next two days home nursing his wounds. He has ice bags on both of his eyes which are swollen along with his face to twice their normal size. He decides he has to end this once and for all.

He calls Luigi and says, "I have pictures of the beating your guys gave me, and if they ever come near me again I am going straight to the police."

Luigi hangs up on Jack, as this is not the news he wanted to hear. He is now forced to call Dominic, his lieutenant who runs Luigi's neighborhood territory.

"Look ,Dominic, dis guy Jack is becoming a loose cannon. He is talking about becoming a canary and singing about us to da cops."

"Okay, Luigi, you did your part. I may call on you to help later after I decide how to handle this situation."

Jack meanwhile feels relieved; he finally told Luigi that he is no longer going to be intimidated by mob's threats. What he doesn't know is that Dominic is on the phone to Carlo looking for permission to head off a possible problem by whacking him. Carlo responds to Dominic, for a lousy $10K I would not have you take him out, but his threat of going to the cops takes this to a new level. Carlo is feeling much less inhibited with his new crematory scheme. Here is a case where he might have written off the 10Gs just to keep the peace. However, now he yearns to get back the old respect on the street that lately seemed to be lost.

"You have my permission to whack Jack. By the way, take Enrico and Luigi along since they already know him; then use our new procedure and call Vinnie he will take it from there. Jack will be given a proper send-off."

"Okay boss; consider it done."

Jack wakes up the next day and again feels insecure. It was too easy to get to him before, how easy would it be for them to do it again? How safe is he now? Jack has a cousin Robby, who is a detective in the NYPD Manhattan Bureau.

He looks up the number of the 16th precinct and asks, "Is detective Robinson in?"

"No, I'm sorry he is off until tomorrow, do you want to leave a message or can someone else help you?"

"No, I'll just call back later thank you."

Jack doesn't know where Robby lives and doesn't want to disturb his aging mother for the number. It can keep until tomorrow he tells himself.

Later that night, Jack is leaving Bozo's after a couple of beers and a good basketball game. On the quiet street late at night walking home he hears an engine noise following him down the street. He turns and sees a black suburban driving slowly and keeping about fifty feet behind him. Jack doesn't need any further clues as to who this could be. He takes off running and cuts a hard right into an alleyway between two buildings. Behind him, he hears car doors open and footsteps getting louder coming from behind. Jack, still being agile, gets to a five foot high gate at the end of the alley and scampers over. He knows this isn't the end of the chase, so he looks for some open space to run towards. On the left is another street and Jack races down the sidewalk. He doesn't see anyone behind him, so he slows his pace and tries to plan his next move. Before he can get his next breath, he sees the black suburban with its lights off barreling down the sidewalk directly towards him. He tries to duck to the right but is hit head on by the left fender of the 6,000 pound SUV. With a sickening thud, his neck is broken and his body is catapulted ten feet into the air.

Luigi jumps out of the back of the Suburban and looks at Jack's mangled body and says, "See what happens when you disrespect us, you lowly piece of shit. We gave youse a chance and you had da balls tu threaten me and my people; you got what you deserve."

Dominic, who is supervising this operation, gives the order, load him up and head for the warehouse boys."

He then calls Vinnie to meet them with the "mortuary van." One more customer for a trip to Pennsylvania. In two more hours, Vic's phone will ring in Duryea, it will be his second operation for the mob.

Success in a Business

IT IS NOW three months since the first *package* arrived in Vic's garage. He has now had three more rendezvous with Vinnie, all as uneventful as the first. With each success and an additional $10,000 into his coffers, Vic is finally a success at a venture. He is careful to not deposit the cash in any of his accounts. He keeps this money literally under his mattress and takes out what he needs to make up payments when he is short in financing the funeral business. Yes, his other business is still a loser, but he can easily now make up the shortfall from his newfound "stash." And it gets better; the extra $40,000 of found money is tax free, which is the reason Vic can't deposit any of this directly into his checking or savings accounts. Only if the IRS were doing a formal audit of Vic's books, would the injections of cash from another source be brought to light.

Given the small size of Vic's funeral business, an IRS audit is not likely. In fact the little money losing funeral home is a perfect dodge to 'launder' the money. Vic is doing in Duryea on a small scale what the mob is doing all across the country on a far larger scale; using legitimate businesses to hide money made in illegal activities. If anything were to go wrong, it would have to happen with the illegal operation of the crematory, and Vic swears to himself this won't happen. With three months in, Vic doesn't even think about a possible snag with these operations. He only has to be around when another call comes in.

It was now time to live a bit. After spending the last several months scraping by from hand to mouth, Vic has a pent up appetite to finally enjoy some of the things he could only dream of before he met Sam. While not rich, Vic has what every American dreams of, excess spendable cash, literally walking around money.

First, Vic takes his eight-year-old minivan with over 100,000 miles on the clock down to the local Chevy dealer. Without ever realizing, he is beginning to look more like a mob member, he purchases a brand new triple black Chevy Suburban with all of the bells and whistles. The truck has a sticker price on the north side of $40,000, but Vic simply puts $10,000 down and finances the rest. *Don't want to show all your new money at one time.* Sitting in his aromatic leather captain's chair driver's seat, Vic is for the first time 'king of the road'.

He now uses his new wheels to take him to the Wilkes-Barre mall and Nugents furniture store. Here he picks out, with the help of a shapely sales assistant, $15,000 worth of cool modern furniture for his man cave. The stuffy looking apartment sparsely furnished with his grandmother's leftovers is to be a thing of the past. Next to the furniture store is Tomorrow's Man, a men's clothier, and another $3,000 for a completely new wardrobe. Finally Vic will look the part of a small town, thirty-year-old capitalist. Vic reflects as he leaves the clothing store with bags of stuff, that this is fun.

"Now I know what I have been missing all this long time in the financial wilderness."

It's funny, but for most people, the stigma of where the money came from soon disappears when one is out enjoying it. Vic is certainly no exception. In one short week, Vic has spent nearly $60,000. But, now with good credit, having paid off his overdue credit cards, he has a whole new outlook on things. Gone are the days when clerks would swipe his credit card and give him that sickening look when the purchase comes back *rejected*. No, life is good, and Vic is going to do what he has to do to keep it that way.

To compliment his living large, Vic, no longer depressed and broke, begins to frequent the local hot spots where the yuppies his age hang out. He can now easily leave tiny Duryea, and appear in Scranton or Wilkes-Barre for his weekends. Vic has regained some of the attitude and momentum he once had in his college days. Vic could order a $50.00 meal, and then stay to dance and party the night away. Combing his hair looking in the mirror, not a bad looking guy, he muses. He's in the pink with proper attire, correct wheels, and the right attitude, combined with being a good spender by buying drinks and leaving good tips at the clubs and bars.

Vic can finally attract the "hot" chicks. He started to hook up with the local girls who frequented these places. He reacquired his taste for dancing and was becoming quite popular with the "in" crowd. After some brief flings with some good looking *women*, Vic begins to realize these relationships always seemed to melt away when they found out what he did for a living. It seems most women aren't thrilled with dating a funeral director, even if he was a *cool* dude. He had to start lying that he was into the computer industry, but that had its limits, and basically Vic was not able to settle in with any one favored lady. He took all this in stride for a while, but he really longed for a *soul mate* to have a permanent relationship with.

Karen

WHEN VIC WAS doing the bar scene in Scranton, one of the bars he stopped at was Basil's. A downtown club on the first floor of a large office building, the modern interior was minimalist almost to being austere. However, Basil's offered a happy hour that went from 4 to 7 p.m., longer than the other Scranton places. On weekends, it also brought in some of the better local bands. Here is where Victor first noticed Karen Schmidt. Karen was one of the more conservatively attired girls in the place; she did not dress especially seductively. But her well-coordinated outfits did show off her curves very well. Besides not being flashy, she hung in the background, not hiding, but not aggressively looking for attention. Vic guessed she was about five foot six, and weighed perhaps one twenty. All of the weight well proportioned. She had a pleasant looking face, not a Hollywood starlet, but better than average. Vic would give her a solid eight.

After a couple of weeks of seeing Karen talk to some of the guys and even do a couple of dances, he ascertained she was not hooked up with any one person. On the fourth visit to Basil's, Vic decides "it's now or never." He will make his move and if she blows him off, well nothing ventured.

Victor was pleased when Karen was not reticent to talk with him and accept a drink from him. She even accompanied him to the dance floor and was pretty agile with that not too shabby body of hers. Vic was impressed. He left it at that, but made it a point to be back the next Friday; there was something about Karen that wasn't there with the other girls he got close to. Vic wanted to get to know this reserved pretty lady better. After more pleasantries the next week, Vic went for broke.

"Karen, I would like to take you to dinner."

"Okay, Vic, where and when?"

"Tomorrow night we will go to Romano's, one of the better Italian restaurants in Old Forge. By the way where do I find you?"

"I live up near the hospital in the Valley View Apartments. Here, I'll write it down for you."

"Tomorrow then, I'll pick you up at six."

Vic was elated, he'd now get a chance to learn more about Karen while having a great meal; life is good.

At dinner the next night Vic learned that Karen is from Wyoming, Pennsylvania, hell right around the corner, and she also graduated Wilkes University with a BA in nursing. She worked at CMC Hospital, the largest in Scranton as an intensive care nurse. "This," thought Vic, "was great, nurses are usually unafraid of the dead because in their hospital training they are marched down to pathology at some point and made to witness an autopsy. That is not for the faint of heart, but hospitals want their nurses used to all aspects of the human body."

After divulging that he ran a funeral home in Duryea none of the usual bad vibes came back from Karen. In fact she seemed genuinely interested and wanted to hear more about Vic's career. At twenty-eight, she was two years younger than Vic, but very mature and a good conversationalist. Victor couldn't believe his luck at finding this near-perfect girl; but there was more than luck at play.

What Vic didn't know was that Karen had been somewhat reticent about meeting other guys, due to an unpleasant experience in her recent past. It seems Karen was dating a doctor at the hospital. Unbeknown to Karen the doctor had a wife back in Philadelphia. All of this came to a head when the little woman came up one Saturday night from the City of Brotherly Love to see why her husband seemed to not want to come home on weekends.

Acting on a tip from a jealous intern at the hospital, Karen and Emily (Mrs. Edward Smallwood) met up in a restaurant in downtown Scranton. This was highly embarrassing to Dr. Smallwood who had one too many women sitting at his table. Karen was mortified, said goodbye, and left that scene forever.

Thus, Karen was free when Vic, through good timing, was observing her. Of course, Vic wanted to get serious immediately, but Karen, coming off of a bad experience was reserved about being intimate with Vic. She wanted to know more about him and feel secure, before she let her emotions get irretrievably involved.

After four weeks, the romance was proceeding like a high school puppy love affair. Vic was hot to engage in any kind of sex he can get, usually settling for kissing and petting in the living room of either his or Karen's apartment.

Karen insisted that she would not sleep with Vic, but was feeling herself getting closer to Vic and actually longing for more. She wanted to be sure, so even though the last time she confided in her mother about a boyfriend it turned out horribly embarrassing for Karen; she needed to know more about Vic.

"Mom, I am dating this funeral director, Victor Kozol. He's a really nice guy from Duryea, but I really don't know much about him, how can I be sure he is who he claims to be?"

"I have a co-worker at the pharmacy where I work who is from Duryea, what if I ask her if she knows anything about Victor?"

"Okay mom, I know it sounds hokey, but I can't get myself emotionally involved for a second time only to find out the other person is an impostor or deeply flawed."

In just one day, Mary Schmidt, Karen's mother is on the phone with her daughter.

"Well Jane, my friend, doesn't know him or his parents who are retired and living in Florida, the rest of his story checks out though. He runs the family funeral home and has never been married. In fact, he only in the last month has been seen in the company of a good looking girlfriend around town."

Karen was ecstatic; she knew that she is that girl. She has in the past couple of weeks been eating out and hanging around Duryea with Vic.

"Oh and Karen, why don't you ask this Victor of yours to come over for a good home cooked meal some Sunday."

"Okay mom, I will see how he reacts to that, and thanks for the help with the 'find out' committee."

In another month, Vic and Karen have spent some nights together both at his place and hers, and they are more enamored with each other than ever. Vic loved the idea of not being lonely, and was happy to shuttle between his place and Scranton. He was actually in love for the first time in his life.

But, as he reflected on the good parts of this new relationship, Victor began to have his own reservations about his future relationship with Karen.

For the first time in months, the other and much darker side of his life started to encroach into his consciousness. There were two elephants in the closet that Victor did not want Karen or anyone else to find out about. One was his funeral business was nearly non-existent; which if and when Karen figured out she might start to wonder, where did Vic get all of the money he had to keep his lifestyle up? This would lead to the much darker secret in Vic's life, his association with underworld characters from New York.

Since Victor never had to associate with them publicly in Duryea, they were separated by one hundred miles of space. This made it much easier to cover for a lifestyle that was anything but normal. But, would the width of the State of New Jersey, forever keep Victor safe from being discovered, especially by Karen?

The Sunday Dinner

IT WAS A gray, overcast fall Sunday the prearranged dinner that Vic has agreed to have with Karen's parents was to take place. He was a little apprehensive about the meeting, but the promise of a roast beef dinner with homemade apple pie took away most of Vic's reservations.

It has been a long time since he has eaten home cooking, and he was not going to back out now. Karen picked him up at 11:00 and drove him over the short distance to Wyoming. The small town of less than five thousand people is much like Duryea but has an area of newer homes up on the hill overlooking the old town. This is where the Schmidts, Mike and Mary, live and also is where Karen was raised. The two story brick home with white trim was neat and well-maintained.

"Welcome to our home, Victor," Mike said as he opened the door and ushered Vic and Karen in. Mary came out from the kitchen with her apron and cutting knife in hand to get her first glimpse of her daughter's new beau.

"I am pleased to meet you, Victor, please feel at home here while I get the meal ready for serving."

"Thanks, Mr. & Mrs. Schmidt, the pleasure is all mine to be here."

"Karen, take Victor into the living room and let him relax for a few minutes while I finish up in here."

"Sure mom."

With that Karen led Vic across the hall into the living room, where, sitting partially obscured from his view behind a protruding bookcase is an older woman. She is Mary's great aunt. Victor stares at Sophie who returns the gaze with equal shock and stands from her chair with amazing agility for a person her age, a spry, wiry athleticism Victor had only ever before witnessed in one other elderly woman.

"He-he-hello, Mrs. Lunitis" stammers Vic.

"Hello Mr. Kozol." Sophie responded with a strong, even tone.

"Fancy meeting you here."

"You know my great Aunt Sophie?" Karen asked amazed.

"We two go way back together in Wilkes-Barre, don't we Victor?" Sophie said with what Victor can only interpret as an evil leer. "Victor was one of my second floor tenants."

"Well, isn't it a small world!" Karen smiled, clapping her hands together in delight.

"Too damned small," Victor thought, "I've got to keep the old bat from talking too much."

"Yes, the best gosh-darned landlady I ever had, too. Okay, she's the only landlady I've ever had, but your Aunt Sophie, she's ..."

Victor wondered how long he can keep up the effusive babbling and opts for a diversionary tactic.

"Well, I guess I better go wash my hands before we start in on this wonderful supper I've been promised."

Sophie didn't reply, but the cat-that-caught-the-canary smile remained.

Sophie will say no more, but the coolness between her and Vic is evident to Karen. Vic knew his dinner was ruined, for Sophie may not destroy him over the dinner table, but when he and Karen leave, it's 'damn the torpedoes'. How to come out of this in one piece is going to be a new Houdini act for Vic. For the present, Vic just sits quietly in the living room talking pleasantries with Mike and Karen.

The dinner was very good, and after some more get acquainted talk Karen and Vic took their leave. Sophie was in the kitchen helping Mary clean up and do the dishes.

"So, you were Vic's landlady back in his college days?"

"Ver do I begin, Victor seems like such a nice Polish boy, but behind that smiling face is a devil. He had the most wild and damaging parties in my building."

Sophie related to Mary how the co-ed fell off the fire escape late one evening and finally how she evicted Vic after her kitchen ceiling fell in from the flood he caused. She spares nothing and even embellishes a few details with a dramatic flourish.

"Victor's father did pay for all the damage, but the mess was terrible," Sophie recounted. She finishes, with "Victor flunked out of Wilkes."

"Well, Sophie," Mary said, "he was young and wild once, we can only hope that now he runs a business and is older and more settled."

"I don't know how he is now, but a few years ago, I would not want him around our family."

"He doesn't seem to have any stopping point built in and he never seems to regret anything that goes wrong. I don't know Mary, it's not my decision, but maybe Karen can find another man. If I were you and Mike, I would have Victor investigated to see how settled he really is."

Mary doesn't want to tell her aunt that she already did some preliminary checking on Vic but couldn't find anything out of order.

Fat Joe

MANY THINK THAT the crime syndicates in New York and elsewhere are constantly fighting turf wars. These organizations or "families" as they are called deal in all types of illegality including drugs, prostitution, gambling, garbage pickup, commercial laundries, and a whole host of other activities. The syndicates act much like public corporations, complete with an established hierarchy and strict rules to be abided by. They do risk management, recruitment, accounting, and all of the things you would think a large business does on a daily basis. The big difference is that you won't find any detailed or published financial reports as you would with most public companies. They share another trait with the legit companies.

They sometimes both engage in monopolistic practices, by carving up the territories into areas of influence. They claim certain territories where they are strongest and cede other areas where they don't have manpower or interest to another syndicate. This has, for years, kept the inter-family wars down to some small brush fights. Only rarely will there be serious upheavals of violence between the syndicates.

Flatbush Avenue in Brooklyn was one of these dividing lines between two families. On the north side, Carlo Dellveccio's family operated, while on the south side of the street, the Rugocci family was in charge. No one knows how long this arrangement prevailed, but it had proven profitable to both families. We all know how keeping discipline in any venture is an imperfect work in progress, sometimes needing fine tuning.

In one particular four square block area, Joe Marucci was in charge for the Rugoccis. He is a mid-level operator sometimes called an 'earner' controlling several 'bag men' (collectors) and 'runners' (money carriers). Joe was not much for running himself, as he was five foot eight and went over three hundred and fifty pounds. He usually sat wedged in his chair in an office behind a small pizza restaurant right on Flatbush Avenue. For whatever reason, Joe's territory is slow this month. His girls are not finding the "johns" at night, the betting is down, and even the drugs are not selling at the rate they normally do. What to do?

Joe sees that across the Avenue there is not much going on. Maybe the Dellveccio guys are on vacation; maybe they lost men and can't man the street anymore. Who knows? All Joe sees is at least a temporary opportunity to send some of his men and girls one hundred feet across Flatbush Avenue and start working the streets over there. Joe knows he should clear this with Marco Rugocci, his boss, but if he says no, then Joe has to report the weak sales and take the heat for that. So, Joe decides to take the matter into his own hands. He sends four of his guys over to distribute drugs through the 'crack heads' who actually do the street sales. He will see what happens and then dispatch the girls to solicit for prostitution next.

For about two weeks, Joe's guys are making sales in the 'forbidden' territory, and there are no repercussions. But on the third week one of Joe's 'soldiers' is severely beaten in an alley behind Flatbush. Worse, some of the drug dealing crack heads can no longer be found on their normal corners.

Joe now has two choices, he can continue to keep doing business over there, or he can pull back to his side of the Avenue. Joe knows that since he didn't consult with Marco first, he can't ask him what to do. Joe decides being a pretty smart guy he is going

Kirby Hall, Wilkes University

Statue of John Wilkes

Chase Hall, Wilkes University

Luzerne County Courthouse, Wilkes Barre

Lackawanna River, Duryea

Holy Rosary Catholic Church, Duryea

Main Street, Duryea

South Main St., Wilkes-Barre

Max Rosen Center, Wilkes Universityniversity

Wilkes Library

Stegmaier Brewery, Wilkes Barre

Weckesser Hall, Wilkes University

Stegmaier Mansion, Wilkes Barre

Breiseth Hall, Wilkes Universityniversity

St. Mary's Polish Nat'l Church, Duryea

to keep 'batting above his average'. He already knows that his counterpart in the Dellveccio family is one Carlos Marini.

Joe asked Carlos to meet with him and maybe they can smooth over some of the ruffled feathers. Carlos responds, "Sure, Joe, we can talk about splitting up the turf maybe a little bit differently. Why don't you come over for dinner tonight at Cataldi's on Third Avenue? Just you and me, Joe, that's how things get done, right, paisano?"

"I'll be there at 8:00 p.m. tonight Carlos, see you then."

Right on time, Joe waddles in and is escorted by Marco to the rear of Cataldi's where a private booth is waiting with wine already poured and the first course of antipasto ready to be served. (It is an old tradition in the mob to first have dinner with or allow one to finish their last meal before you take them out). And that is exactly what Marco has planned.

"Joe, I think we're a little short of help right now, so maybe we can give you the first couple of blocks in from Flatbush right now. After all we can't have your men getting into jams like they did last week by being where they shouldn't have been."

"Sure," Joe says, "I knew you could agree on letting us have a couple of blocks for now; who knows when you need a favor yourself someday? Enjoy."

"Bon appetite."

With Cannoli and cappuccino served last, Marco says, "Joe, let's go out to my car and we'll drive the area you had in mind. After we agree on the streets we can shake on it."

Joe is ecstatic; he never knew that negotiating between the families could be so easy.

"My Lincoln is behind the kitchen, let's go out this way."

When Joe and Marco get out into the dark alleyway, he is jumped by three of Marco's boys, knocked unconscious and thrown in the back of a waiting van. A familiar ritual is repeated with the van driving to the docks and an abandoned warehouse at the end of one of the piers. When they get inside it takes four guys to remove Joe from the van and dump him into a chair.

Splashing him with a bucket of cold water to revive him, Marco says "Did you think we just got off the banana boat, Joe? You think you can just move into someone's territory because you want it? Well Joe, unfortunately it doesn't work that way, and I'm afraid you flunked your first and last test in management negotiating," roars Marco.

Joe is flushed, shaking, and profusely sweating. "Okay, Marco, I was wrong, I'll pull my guys off and we'll go back to business as usual on our own sides of the street tomorrow."

"No, Joe, that's not how this is going to end." With that Marco pulls out a suppressed 9 mm Glock 19 and puts three shots through Joe's heart. Next, the call goes out to Vinnie to bring his van, but Marco tells him, "Make sure you ate your Wheaties today." After much struggling Joe barely fits into the pouch, but the zipper is overstressed and jams trying to close it. Four men struggle with the handles on the pouch as they muscle it into Vinnie's van for the trip to Duryea. Except for Joe's weight, it all seemed routine at the time. No one knew that Joe, inadvertently through his overeating, would wreck a scheme that took almost a year to set-up.

Fat Joe the Fifth Case for Victor

A WEEK AFTER the family dinner at the Schmidt's, Vic and Karen are dining out on a crisp and cool Friday night in Old Forge at Verna's; another one of the many fine restaurants in this town of eateries.

Karen tells Vic, "You know Auntie Sophie wants my parents to do a full investigation of you; you must have really made some impression on her when you were at college."

With that a chill goes down Vic's spine, an investigation, even if they are not serious, sets off alarm bells throughout his brain.

"Why would they do that, Karen? I'm just a small town funeral director trying to make a living like everyone else. Look, I admit I was pretty crazy in college. Your Aunt and I used to mix it up regularly over the weekend parties in my apartment. But it was just the old "sowing your wild oats thing." There was nothing sinister or criminal, just a bunch of college kids for the first time away from home letting off steam. That's not who I am now, we all mature and leave that lifestyle behind. At least I sure did."

"Don't be so defensive, Vic. I know what college was like. I just didn't have it as easy as you because I had to live at home and commute every day to classes. But you know the older generation will never look the other way when they see the type of carrying on that students do. It's okay with me, Vic, I didn't even know you back then. You don't have to justify your actions from ten years ago, just what you do now."

But for the first time Victor's outburst about his past leaves Karen feeling a bit uneasy, *Does Vic protest too much?*

Her mind then turns to the great unknown about Vic. "Where does he get all of the money he seems to never run short of? Is it an inheritance; is his funeral business actually better than it seems? Who is Vic's secret financial angel? She dated more than a couple of guys in her time, and none ever had the endless resources of Vic. There was always that time the guy was short and she would go 'Dutch treat'. But never with Vic."

All of these thoughts were cut short when Vic's cell phone rang. Vic, to not disturb the other diners and make sure he was out of earshot of Karen, walks over to the lounge to answer it. Karen thinking that it was a death call (it really was that) became all excited.

Vic says, "Karen, we have to finish up here and leave I have business to attend to."

"I want to come along," she says. "I can lift my end of the stretcher; I'll be your assistant in the removal of the body."

Normally if this were just that a 'death call', Victor would not have minded taking Karen along. After all there is no law against having unlicensed staff assisting funeral directors in their duties. But, this was not a normal call and Vic was not about to have Vinnie from New York ever come into contact with Karen. She was too quick on the uptake not to realize that this operation Vic was going on was no normal death call pick-up in a small town or for that matter any funeral director. Vic had to think of something quickly, something he rarely had to do lately.

There was this time at Wilkes University, where he inadvertently invited two different girls to come to his apartment on the same night and party. He knew these girls weren't into 'tricycling', so he had to feign an illness with one, by throwing up in the cafeteria right in front of her. Oh well, not classy, but she got the message and stayed away. But, poetic justice came into play and the other girl didn't show up either. However, this was far more serious than two acquaintances overpopulating his apartment.

Flash back to present. "Look Karen, That was Geissinger Hospital, Mrs. Smerkosky just died, but I can't get her body until tomorrow after the autopsy. There really isn't anyone to pick up tonight, but I might have to talk to her family later on."

"You mean after 10:00 p.m. you are going out to see them?"

"Oh yes, we funeral directors give our families that kind of personalized service."

"Okay, but count me in for next time." (If only she knew how long it was between death calls in Vic's business.)

"Sure, but you can still stay with me at my place tonight."

"I'm on for that."

Whew, there is one problem with having a steady relationship with someone, they are around a lot. Sometimes they are around just too much. But then Vic thought of the brighter side of cuddling up with this nubile young nurse tonight after his 'little duty' was done, it all seemed worthwhile. The second call came while Vic was at his place watching TV with Karen. He knows that the 'shipment' is within fifteen minutes of his garage again.

"It's time for me to go over and see the family," says Vic as he heads out the door.

Vic arrived at the garage, and shortly thereafter the black van arrived and pulled into the darkened space. Vic hits the close button for the overhead door. It again went as planned, the garage swallowed up the van and its contents away from all prying eyes. Tonight something is different; three guys get out of the van, Vinnie and two strangers. It seems that this 'shipment' is much heavier than before and would be too much for Vic and Vinnie to muscle into the retort. With two guys in the van at one end and

Vic and Vinnie outside trying to take the head end, they slowly slide Fat Joe out of the van. Then with a crash, the pouch hits the floor. Once more all four guys grab the handles on the side of the pouch and collectively let out a large grunt lifting the body into the retort.

"What did this guy eat, bricks? He must go over three hundred pounds."

No one answers Vic as the now sweaty crew climbs back into the van while Vinnie hands Vic his envelope. Then they depart for New York.

A body of this size could take over two hours to incinerate and Vic has other plans for the evening. He was determined to not get into bed with Karen already asleep. He tried that once before, she never woke up and he had to go to sleep frustrated. That was not going to happen tonight.

Vic pushes the buttons to start the retort. This will kick in a program which will ramp up the heat until 1,600 degrees is reached and then maintain that temperature for a set period, and finally go into cool down mode. Vic has to wait to call his 'fire stop' code in until later as they know he can't cremate and dispose of the body that quickly. He hangs around a few minutes to make sure everything is alright then heads back in his Suburban for the funeral home. On his way out he notices an odd jet engine sound coming from the three foot in diameter six foot high galvanized pipe extending through the roof that is the hot air duct that finally releases the purified gases generated in the furnace to the atmosphere.

Vic says to himself, "Boy machine, you got a job on your hands tonight."

Vic has timed it right; Karen has just gone to bed. With her being away on night shift for the last week, both were in a mood to begin where they last left off with the serious business of love making. After a protracted period of phenomenal sex, both he and Karen drift off to sleep.

Just as Vic is going into a sounder sleep he is awakened by the shrill sound of fire engine sirens in the distance. Not to worry, he thinks the only thing over there is "my garage." Victor suddenly remembers in one of the Chicago classes on operating retorts where he was half-dozing off, there was a special emphasis on treating severely obese bodies that weigh over three hundred pounds.

What can happen said the instructor is that there is too much fatty tissue. Instead of burning at a controlled rate, the fat erupts in a tremendous inferno overflowing the tray lip the body is resting in. The excess burning liquid fat is carried by the fans up the flue and into the exhaust pipe on the roof. From here the burning fat overflows and starts the roof on fire. If not caught in time, the entire building could be destroyed. "At least the deceased gets his wish and is cremated," Vic thought. The instructor remarks, there have been more than a couple of crematories burned to the ground by an out of control, hard to extinguish fat fire. The proper procedure was for the operator to stay by the retort and manually start and stop the burner so that the fire burns slowly and doesn't do the above. The key warning, don't leave the retort alone. "Yikes, I did this."

Victor's entire life flashes in front of him as he races to the garage.

"Oh God, how do I explain this?"

Vic thinks the simple way out is to call it an accident. The scenario of an empty retort starting itself by reason of a faulty connection or error in the computer circuit boards is the way he has to spin it. So far so good. Vic could pass a lie detector test on the fact it was an accident. But, if they ever ascertained that someone was in the retort, who was it in there when it went out of control? As the operator, he was not only supposed to know, but have a cremation permit from the state.

Vic had no Department of Vital Statistics papers for that body. He didn't know who was in there or have a permit; this is not good. "Let's see . . . an anonymous fat person from out of state started a fire in a crematory he wasn't authorized to be in. This is pretty damning for the owner-operator," thought Vic.

The only good news so far is that Vic knows the fireman who tell him that with all of this heat there can be no investigation until later in the day or even after that. Vic knows, he would be a lot safer if he could somehow get the remains of that body out of the retort chamber, before any investigator looks in there. Then Vic would have a chance to make his theory of a malfunction causing the machine to overheat believable. Anything is better than finding a body in the main chamber of the retort.

Vic now has a splitting headache from the heat of the fire and mental exhaustion thinking about the jam he has gotten himself into. Even though the firemen turned off the natural gas and electricity to the garage, the flames still are licking fifty feet into the night sky. The fire has a mind of its own and keeps on burning. Fortunately, no one lived in that block and there wouldn't be any casualties from Vic's mistake. If that happened, it would be called criminal negligence, Vic recalled from his old funeral law classes. This is what it is called when you are careless or negligent and others are injured and killed. Vic after first sweating is now shivering in the cold night air.

He tells his old friend Chief Willis, he has no idea how it started and was home sleeping when he heard the sirens. At least that part was true. The chief told him it will take all night to put the fire out, and after that it will be so hot that no one will be able to get near it for several hours, if not a day' to investigate. Victor hoped so.

Daybreak came, after watching the fire most of the night except for one break when he went home to tell Karen, Vic was more anxious than ever to know what was in the retort. How much was left of the body, could there be enough to be identified? These were questions Vic had to know the answers to, and soon. The building, while still smoldering and emitting some smoke into the air, was now a five foot high pile of rubble. You could make out the burned out hulks of the two old funeral cars in the corner, and the large steel framework of the retort still stood in the middle of the floor. Since the firebrick that lined the chambers of the retort were still intact you could not see inside the chamber holding the body. Vic mused, how to find out what lies inside the mystery chamber? Chief Willis's main concern was that no person was working, staying in, or walking by the building at the time. Vic assured the chief that no one was inside at the time of the fire. (At least no one who was alive, but the chief didn't ask that question.)

The chief would have known that all funeral and embalming operations were handled across town at the funeral home, but what about that new crematory? The chief didn't think to ask and Vic stayed mum on the subject. There were going to be some serious questions to answer for in the not too distant future. There would be a fire marshal, who will ask about the crematory, and then there was New York. What to tell Sam about this? How will the organization react to mistakes by their associates? Vic will just have to roll with these punches as they come.

Digging Out

BY 6:00 A.M. Vic is back at the funeral home apartment. He is watching Karen get dressed and glad to see her leave so that he can do some serious thinking. "

Well, Karen, the garage and crematory are gone, but luckily no one got hurt. I will be busy handling all of the details created by this in the next couple of days; so I probably won't be able to call you until later in the week."

"Since you're so distracted with the fire, maybe I can help you with the Smerkosky funeral that came in last night.

"Oh no thanks, but I got that covered, next time you will be my number one assistant."

With that Karen leaves for her shift at the hospital and Vic is left to prioritize his next actions.

"There are certainly bone fragments in the retort from last night's cremation of his mystery case from New York," Vic theorizes.

If they could only disappear, then the fire can be something else or even undetermined origin.

Vic calls his friend Chief Wills to find out the status of the garage site. Wills says it is up to the State Fire Marshall to come down from Dunmore to determine the cause. But since the site is still hot, he is scheduled to arrive tomorrow. For now the chief has had the site cordoned off with yellow danger zone tape. Vic would love to go right over, but not now, it is still too hot and there is too much light. His plan is to wait until dark and then go over to retrieve the remains.

On the second question of calling Sam in New York, Vic will hold off on that until he has the situation here under control. No sense prematurely bringing who knows what down on himself.

At 10:00 p.m. Vic takes a cardboard box, a broom, and a small shovel with him to the garage site. He parks outside the bright yellow tape line, and crosses in with a flashlight in hand. Going straight to the front of the retort, he finds the steel doors are warped but intact. Because the hydraulic fluid that operates the door has evaporated with the fire, the doors pry open easily with the help of the shovel. Just as he expected, the skeletal remains of 'John Doe' are in the chamber, the rest of the body was consumed in the enormous fire. Vic sets the box on the ground in front of the open doors and begins to sweep and shovel the remains into the box. The large bones from the legs and arms are brittle and they crush easily and fit into the box. Vic now sweeps out what is left and then scatters a few light ashes to cover the sweep marks. He then closes the door and smudges up the scratch marks on the doors made by the shovel, and closes the box. Just as he is returning to his SUV, two bright lights pierce the darkness of the deserted street. It is one of the two Duryea police cars, Vic panics, puts the box down just as a cop with a blinding flash light barks, "Who goes there?"

"It's me, Victor Kozol the owner."

The cop now recognizes Vic as a former high school classmate that he once hung out with. Ned O'Brien says, "Vic what are you doing here this late?"

"Oh hi, Ned. I called my parents in Florida to let them know about the fire and my mother said there were some heirlooms of hers that may still be in the garage, and would I try and retrieve them for her."

"Did you find them, Vic?"

"I found very little, just a couple of metal picture frames that didn't burn, but at least it's something."

Vic's heart is still pounding. If Ned says open the box, it's all over.

"Okay, no one is supposed to contaminate the site until the fire marshal gets here tomorrow, but you're the owner so go ahead."

Vic is sweating under his coat, as his old friend leads him back out to his SUV. "That was close and one advantage of living in a small town; if that had happened in Scranton, I would be toast," Vic thought.

Vic returned to the funeral home and with a hammer pulverized the rest of the bones that remain. The electric pulverizer called a processor was of course lost in the fire. Finally, it is off to the Main Street bridge over the Lackawanna River Vic where he dumps the lumpy contents of his box into the swirling waters below. His immediate tasks complete, he goes home and relaxes, but not completely, because he still has to deal with Sam in New York. Vic figures, he might as well tell him straight on.

With that, he picks up the phone and dials Sam's private number. Sam answers groggily, "This better be important waking me up after midnight."

"It is, Sam; we lost the crematory last night."

"How can you lose a piece of machinery that weighs ten tons, Vic?"

"It was destroyed in a fire."

"Didn't you just get a 'shipment' from us last night?"

"Yes, and that part went alright, I took care of business for you and then went to bed, after that the fire occurred."

"Your version of this better be right, Vic, because this is certainly bad news."

Vic asks, "Where do we go from here?"

"Look I will have to talk to my investors and see what we can do about this. In the meantime, I hope you have insurance for the loss."

"Of course I do, but for now we are out of business with the crematory."

"Keep me posted, Vic, and try to keep the publicity down, I'll get back to you as to our next move."

"So long, Sam." Victor hangs up.

Now Sam, who has been quite the star with his 'firestop' project has to tell Carlo and the others that they are no longer able to make bodies disappear from New York. Unlike the last few dinner meetings at Rosselli's, this one was not going to be good for Sam.

At Sam's portion of the business meeting the news was received as he already knew it would be, with great shock and anger. In the last few months, the project had taken five bodies out of the investigations, and made sure that several members of the family were not going to be prosecuted for their crimes. No one other than this select group of 'made men' knew where the bodies were going, but everyone else was sure they weren't in the New York City Medical Examiner's Office for autopsies and evidence collection. This had given them a freer hand to eliminate problems in the past year.

The agreement around the table was to try to resurrect the program in the quickest possible time. Sam was directed to investigate what went wrong in Pennsylvania and see if the old program could be restored with rebuilding or must a new approach be taken. Sam further was given the authority to punish Vic if it comes out that his carelessness caused this to happen. Meanwhile, it was decided that termination orders for several deadbeats and canaries that were pending, but not pressing, would be put on hold until this wrinkle could be ironed out. Meeting adjourned 11:10 p.m.

The next day Vic was pacing around his apartment. "The more problems I solve, the more keep coming at me. I guess I don't live right," Victor blurts out to no one in particular.

There are now three fires to put out coming out of the one two nights ago. First, the fire marshal is going to be combing through that pile of rubble across town and trying and find out what really happened to start the fire. Second, he has to wait to hear from Sam about what they are going to do about the lost crematory. He doesn't expect this to be a friendly confrontation. Third and worst of all, he has to pick up his father, who is now on a plane from Fort Lauderdale to Avoca, the local airport. He of course wants to know what happened to some of his now charcoaled real estate. What if he stumbles onto the fact that over half of the clientele that he left in Victor's hands are now at the competitors? None of which are going to be good!

Life isn't fair; I never wanted this damned business in the first place. My two cousins are living the good life downstate as doctors and here I am stuck in this place. Maybe I should have studied when I had a chance in college; too late for that now; the old man's plane lands in an hour.

Albert Kozol has Victor cornered in the tiny first floor office in the rear of the funeral home. "What the hell happened to a garage that stood for seventy years until you got hold of it."

"I don't know, Dad, but that's why they have fire insurance, because no one knows when or where a fire will break out."

"Was it the gas in those two old Cadillacs we stored there?"

"Dad, like I've been saying, we won't have any answers until the fire marshal does his investigating."

"Other than that, have you been busy with funerals?"

"Well you know it's always been feast or famine. Sometimes I could use four guys to help me, other times, like now, it is slow."

"Hmm, well at least after I raised hell with you the last time, you are sending my checks on time, so I guess business can't be too bad. However, some of our old friends say it's not the same since I left."

"Dad, they always say that when a younger generation takes over, they naturally yearn for the good old days."

"Take me to the garage, I want to see it.

What the hell is that huge steel box on the floor son?"

"That's our new crematory retort."

"Where did you get the money to buy that?"

"Easy, it's leased. See, Dad, it's the modern way, you have to keep up with the times. The younger generation doesn't want burials anymore, and it is helping pay the rent to you." (If only Albert knew how much of the rent the retort was paying.)

"Okay, but what if that furnace took the building down?"

"Dad, I keep telling you, we don't know that yet, and besides there's insurance."

"I've seen enough, we can go to dinner tonight and I'll be flying out on the 7:10 a.m. flight back to Fort Lauderdale."

"I just wanted you to be satisfied with everything, Dad."

The next morning Vic drove his father to the airport and breathed a sigh of relief; Dad was too disturbed by the fire to look at the books of the business or call up any friends to 'chew the fat' with. Thank god for that, now onto the next problem.

Mike Shoemaker had been with the Pennsylvania State Police for twenty years, rising through the ranks from a highway patrol trooper for ten years and the last ten investigating fires. Mike has seen them all in his career which took him all over the Commonwealth.

"So here we have an old, free standing, garage with one of those new pre-packaged crematory retorts standing in the middle of it. And that's the area where it looks like it started.

Mike knew these units could have fat fires, particularly if they were overloaded. They could also erupt if the chimney flue was blocked. A funeral home in Philadelphia and two in Pittsburgh lost parts of their buildings in just such fires. The cause of two was that the retort was overloaded with an extra heavy body, which overheated the flue and the fire spread to the surrounding structure. The third was a tree fell on top of the flue and blocked the exhaust.

But, upon opening the retort doors at Vic's garage, there were no remains in the chamber. Normally this evidence points to a fat fire, but where is the body? Mike will have to interview the owner after he is sure of the facts.

He makes a call to the Perfectall Manufacturing Company in Chicago Illinois, builder of the retort. After identifying himself, he asks to speak to one of their engineers. Tom Haskell quality control engineer gets on the phone with Mike, after hearing Mike's initial findings, he says. "We have never had any combustion in one of our units that wasn't set into operation by the operator. The units can only go into a combustion mode by pressing the three buttons on the control panel. Never had a unit self-ignite by some kind of short circuit or electrical malfunction. We just have too many backups designed into the product."

As to fires once the unit was operating, Tom tells Mike exactly what he already knew about oversized bodies and blocked flues. Mike also knew that there was a manual override procedure taught at the operator classes for dealing with that. Mike thanks Tom for telling him about the electrical circuitry and the other part about fat fires. This almost certainly ruled out any new reason for a retort to start combustion on its own. Mike needed to be sure so he would still get an independent electrical engineer to check the circuits to make sure that the safeguards Tom said were in place and operational.

The only other lead he had to pursue was to get Victor Kozol's take on what happened, as he was apparently the last one to use the retort and was legally responsible for it.

Victor smiled and sat Mike down in his small office.

"As you can see we run a pretty tight operation here, I'm pretty much it around here."

Mike begins, "When was the last time you used the retort?"

"Let's see" looking through his cremation permits, "here it is three weeks ago we had John Halobosky cremated."

"You only used the crematory once in three weeks?"

"Yes, it's been slow here of late; I wish I was busier."

"You don't do any outside business with other funeral directors or let them operate your retort?"

"Heavens no, they don't like me because I'm a competitor, and I would never let an outsider touch my equipment."

"Okay, Vic, I guess that's all for now, but could you make me a copy of the cremations you did this year?"

"Sure, I have it right here, give me a second to get it and you can take it with you."

Victor wasn't sure how this interview went. Shoemaker has no evidence of additional bodies including the big one the other night. However, he doesn't seem ready to call it a short circuit or some other thing like a lightning strike either. Just have to wait and hope he gets some more interesting fires to investigate and goes away.

The next chore was for Vic to meet with his insurance representative Charley Kranovick. Charley asks Vic to stop over to his office.

"The good news is that your father had the building fully insured and you have been keeping up with the premiums. It looks like a total loss and you will be getting about $60,000 to rebuild. However, you never called me to put the crematory retort on the coverage. That is too major of an item to be covered under contents; it would have needed a separate rider for inclusion on the master policy."

"You mean I still owe for a machine that is now destroyed?"

"I'm sorry, Vic, it is the policy holder's obligation to notify me of any additions or changes to their policy."

Vic now knows that the co-signers on the lease who are Sam's "investors" are on the hook for replacing the $50,000 retort. This is not what he disclosed to Sam in that brief telephone exchange yesterday. All of this will have to be faced head-on with Sam in the not too distant future.

Sam

AT 5:00 A.M. the next morning the doorbell began intruding into Vic's dream. He is now half-awake with a hangover from last night's downing of a six pack to dull the pain from all of his troubles. Yes, it is the doorbell, not the dream; and it won't stop.

"Who in the hell is here in the middle of the night; and what can be so important to disrupt the only peace I ever see on this planet?"

The ring is now a steady unrelenting noise getting louder in Vic's addled brain. He has no choice but to grab his slippers and robe and head for the front door downstairs.

Vic cracks open the door in his stupor and is pushed violently back as the door swings in crashing against the wall behind it.

"What the hell is this?"

With that, Vinnie spins Vic around and frog marches him back to his office where he is unceremoniously dumped into his chair. The chair is then spun around to face Vinnie and a snarling Sam.

"After your phone call, I did some checking on retort fires, Vic, it seems you screwed up; not the machine. Since you lied to me, it's now personal.

You have now embarrassed me in front of my people in New York. I can take the heat, Vic, but can you? You see, this is more than just saving face; it is financial, and people get hurt when a lot of money is lost. How do you think those unnamed bodies in those pouches you cremated got there in the first place? Did you ever stop to think that some of them might have owed the same associates that loaned you money?"

Vic is scared, and wants all of this just to go away. "Look, Sam, I think this is a good time to let bygones be just that and we go our separate ways. I'll take my losses and you take yours and we simply part company as friends."

With that, Vinnie smacks Vic with a backhand to the face that spins the office chair around in a complete circle.

"What the hell did you do that for?"

"Just to get your attention, Vic, you seemed to be a little unfocused. Now that I have your attention, we can proceed like the businessmen that we are."

"Yah, but . . ."

Wham, another couple of blows to the face sends Vic's chair in the other direction and he is now woozy from all the hits. In this instant, Vic finally is forced to bring to his consciousness what he always knew and has been repressing for months, that he is cremating and destroying evidence of murdered victims for the New York mob.

Vic no longer has the luxury of the one hundred miles of distance from New York to protect him from his 'investors'. All of these past months, he was living the good life never caring where the money was coming from. He is now looking straight into the eyes of the source of that money. Not having a hangover anymore, Vic now feels a new emotion, pure, raw fear for himself and his future.

"Now listen up. This is what's going to happen, Vic. You are going to take your insurance money and rebuild the crematory as fast as possible. You are going to open for business again normally, and be ready to receive 'shipments' from us again. Further, because of your negligence with my associate's money, that they so graciously lent you, when you were 'up against a wall financially' you are going to assume some new duties."

"New what," Vic whimpers.

"You will take that shiny new suburban that my friends and I paid for and make pickups in New York for us, instead of us driving the 'shipments' here to you."

"What? I never agreed . . ."

Thump, a fist goes into Vic's stomach and he double over in pain falling out of the chair and crashing onto the floor.

"Well now you are agreeing; are we clear on that?"

"Yah, Sam, Vic gasps. But why the tough guy ruffing up?"

"What could happen to you next, could make this seem like child's play, Vic, that's why. Now, I don't want you hurt nor do you want to be hurt. So, man up and pay your debts by getting on board with the program. This is all I am going to say on this matter. I want progress reports on your rebuilding schedule, and finally, I expect to hear that you are operational and ready to come to New York. That's all, goodbye, Vic. Oh, and by the way, you have a cute little playmate, Karen, I think is her name."

Vic hears the door close, and after a few minutes crawls up on all fours slowly and painfully getting back into his chair. Vic is now terrified for himself and Karen.

Hitting Bottom

THE NEXT MORNING didn't bring any cheer to Vic. He was even more miserable than he had ever been in his entire life, and that's saying a lot. Physically, he felt like he had been hit by a bus, and that might be the better part of his situation. His deteriorating relationship with New York was brought to this point by Sam figuring out what actually happened to the retort. Vic began wondering how long it would take the fire marshal to come to a similar conclusion. You add this to the one part Sam doesn't know, he doesn't have the nearly $50,000 needed to pay off the lease for the destroyed retort since it was uninsured.

There seemed to be only two possible outcomes from all of this; he could go to jail for a whole raft of criminal acts, or be killed or maimed by the mob for screwing up the operation.

Vic now answers the phone and it's Karen on the 'find out committee' wondering why she hasn't seen much of him lately.

"Look, Karen, the fire really has me down right now. I just don't think I would be good company."

Vic fails to mention that he might be dangerous company to hang around with right now. Sam already knew about his parents in Florida, he now also knows about Karen. No one connected to me is safe in this situation Vic reasons.

But Karen insists, "I'll come over tonight, make us something to eat and we can just chill out."

Vic is truly lonely so he replies, "Okay, but don't expect to find me in a good mood."

Vic goes over to the mirror, and for the first time since the altercation gets a look at himself.

"Oh my god, I look like one of those hockey players coming off the ice after a fight, how do I keep this from Karen?" He picks up the phone to cancel out Karen, but can't bring himself to do it, and drops the phone back onto the cradle. Vic is trapped.

Karen is shocked when she gets her first good look at Vic.

"What happened to you?"

"I tripped on the throw rug at the top of the stairs and tumbled down, but nothing appears to be broken." *At least for now.*

Karen gets closer to survey the damage; she is much too astute to believe Vic's answer; "You look like people we get in the hospital on weekends after a barroom brawl."

"Well I can assure you I wasn't in any barroom fighting."

Karen lets it drop until after they eat and Vic has a couple of beers to relax him. Karen opens up with, "Vic I can tell something big is going on here; you have always been tight lipped about your life, but you are really closed down right now."

"I know. It's just an accumulation of everything that's happened lately. I just feel trapped and defeated."

"Look after any storm, no matter how severe, the sun always shines."

Vic knows that neither he nor Karen have ever seen this kind of storm.

"Want to talk about this?"

"I don't want to get anyone else, especially you, getting involved in my self-made troubles."

"Why not?"

"Because there could be consequences. And if you had nothing to do with any of it, why should I ensnare you into it?"

"Vic, this is getting really weird, what situation and ensnared how? Aren't we two people who care very much about each other trying to get our arms around a problem that might be too big for either one of us alone?"

"If only it were that simple Karen."

"Are you going to open up, or am I going to be forever shut out of your life?"

"Did you ever hear the expression 'If I tell you I'll have to kill you'?" Well, what if I tell you and someone else will have to kill you?"

"This conversation keeps going in circles Vic. Who is going to kill whom in Duryea Pennsylvania?"

"Karen, you don't have to be someone important to get killed like the Kennedys and Martin Luther King. Ordinary people can get into a situation that can get them killed."

"Wow, you are evasively telling me that you are involved in something very dangerous."

"If I get specific, you will be involved too. Knowledge is power, but it can also be damning."

"Vic, I still want to know, I'll take my chances on being damned."

"You may be sorry you insisted, but here it is."

For the next thirty minutes Vic recounts his very unhappy life starting with college, getting stuck with a business he let fail, and finally meeting the mysterious lawyer in Atlantic City. How his financial debacle made him turn to people he would have never dreamed of associating with. Finally, describing the terrible liability he has become to himself, his family and even her.

"It isn't pretty, but you can leave now, since anyone with a half a brain would want to put plenty of distance between me and them after they heard that story. I wish any part, or all of it, weren't true. But, that's the way it is Karen. I only wish that you would walk away in silence. If you don't your life could be in jeopardy, especially if they thought you knew what I just told you."

"Vic, you don't think I asked you to open up to me so that I could just walk out on you? I love you. The test of any relationship is going through the tough times together. But if I stay, you have to promise me that you will accept my help to get you out of this."

What help, you going to bake a cake with a file in it so I can break out of my maximum security cell?"

"No, but there was a way in; so there has to be a way out of this."

"Sure, Karen, I call Chief Sarensky down at boro hall and say you're not going to believe this. He would say you're right, I don't believe it, and perhaps you are just covering for a fire you caused on your own property. The local police won't be able to protect me or touch those guys all the way back in New York."

"You may be right on that, Vic. But, I was thinking of something else. My mother's brother, John Flaherty, lives in Philadelphia and is a senior agent with the FBI."

"The FBI, are you crazy? That's like . . . overkill."

"Is it, Vic? Let's see, you have murder, interstate commerce, destruction of evidence, conspiracy, and more all wrapped up here."

Vic thought, "Not bad for a nurse to rattle off all of those technical charges."

"You mean you bring in Uncle John. I tell him what I just revealed to you and he cuffs me and hauls me back to Philly to rot in jail?"

"No, Vic, there are deals people make with law enforcement where the lesser guys turn evidence on the higher-ups who are the real criminals. The low level guy gets probation or a fine and the *big fish*, who masterminded everything, gets prosecuted for the major crimes and does real jail time."

"I guess I can see myself in witness protection, wearing a wig on a desert island, waiting for some hit man to whack me."

"Vic, if you do nothing, you won't have to worry about that. They already found you; just look at that face. I would say you have been warned. The next time they come you may be in your own morgue downstairs; you have to preempt them and move first."

The FBI

AT 9:00 A.M. the next day Karen called her Uncle John in Philadelphia from a friend's house. She spent several minutes recounting, as best she could recollect, this one of a kind story.

Later that same day Agent John contacted Vic at the number Karen had given him. "Listen, Vic, don't say anything just write this down. Take Karen's car and get on the northeast extension of the turnpike heading south. Exit at Allentown and head west on Route 22 to Route 100. Look for the Holiday Inn Hotel. When you get there go directly to room 401. Leave right now."

Karen had already taken Vic's suburban to work and left the keys for her Toyota behind. One hour later, upon turning off Route 100, Vic sees two signs. Left is for the Stroh brewery tour and right is to the hotel. Ahead is the five story brick brew house. Vic knows where he would rather go.

Finding room 401, Vic is greeted by a tall red haired fiftyish looking guy in a gray suit. This is agent John Flaherty, Karen's uncle. Standing next to him is a younger, taller guy in another gray suit looking equally as official. This is Agent Robert Kleckner.

"Come on in, Vic. Coffee?"

"No thanks, I'm not thirsty right now."

Agent Flaherty directs Vic to a green upholstered chair and the two agents sit on a love seat opposite him.

"First, Vic, I believe your story. We were quite surprised that the notorious DellVeccio family has penetrated Pennsylvania for the first time in our memory. For this I take personal offense, because now they are operating in my territory."

John further knows that the mob is getting a lot of heat in New York from prosecutors like Giuliani and a newly energized, non-Hoover FBI. It was J Edgar who never seemed to want to go head-to-head with organized crime. It was even alleged that Hoover, being a major horse track gambler himself, was 'in bed' with some crime figures. John knew these days of avoiding mob crime were over and he would not get resistance from higher ups in the agency if he mounted this investigation. It might, if successful, even get him a promotion. He continues. "Getting rid of incriminating evidence, especially bodies of people they have offed, has always been a high priority of crime families. So, I am not shocked that you were enlisted to help in one of their operations."

"Now, as to your involvement, Vic, I can't promise immunity from prosecution or any deal at this time. We simply know too little about this scheme to talk particulars. In fact, we only know the second-hand story from my niece at this point. What I will say, if all of this proves to be true and you help us, we will go to the proper authorities at the appropriate time and try to work out the most favorable deal possible for you."

So, Vic recounts for the two agents all he knows of the DellVeccio syndicate through his contacts with Sam and Vinnie. He fleshes in the details of the general story Karen already told them.

"Okay," Vic says, "I told you everything I know. Keep me posted on how it works out, see you guys later."

"Not so fast, Vic, we have very little to go on here. First, all of the bodies and their remains have been destroyed by the cremations you performed. Even any ashes are long gone into the

Chesapeake Bay by now. And the fire that destroyed your crema-
torium has wiped out any forensic evidence we could get there.
We will link up with Mike Shoemaker the Fire Marshall to see
what evidence he has, but we don't think any of it will trace back
to the DellVeccios in New York. Let's face it, any evidence we
have traces back to you only, Vic."

"I knew I shouldn't have come. My situation is hopeless. I'll
just have to take my chances. Thanks anyway guys."

"Vic, again, you're jumping to conclusions here. I didn't say we
could never reach the people who set you up, but we probably
can't get to them without your help."

"Hey, John, really that's all I know. Can't you use your Dick
Tracy wrist radio and put out a warrant for their arrest and round
them all up?"

"Like I said earlier, Vic, round them up for what? We need for
you to re-establish contact with Sam and Vinnie so that we can
catch them in the act of illegally disposing of a body they have
murdered."

"You mean I pretend everything is still kosher with them, and
try to trap them?"

"Something along those lines, Vic."

"This option sounds more dangerous for me than keeping
them happy."

"Vic, now that we know about it, that option for you is gone.
We either have to prosecute you for what you say you did, or cut
a deal with you to go after the big fish."

"Somehow I knew there was more to this than just driving
down here and talking."

Vic is conflicted when he leaves the hotel for the return trip
to Duryea. He can see light at the end of the tunnel, once Sam,
Vinnie, and the others are locked up. But, he also knows any

wrong moves while dealing with them and that light at the end of the tunnel could be an oncoming train.

Just as when he got into this bad deal, he is now in with the law in an effort to extricate himself from Sam and company. In two days the FBI sets up a command center at the Woodlands on Route 315 about five miles from Duryea. Vic is called in for the first meeting on Monday morning. He is now sitting in a hotel room at the hotel with Agents John and Robert, plus a third guy they call Gus. Gus is an electronics guru who is manning computers and a tape recorder set up on a long table.

"Vic, before we get into this, are you ready to take a lie detector test?"

"Sure, Bob, anything you say to get this done."

"Okay, this will come later, but for right now we have to give you your introductory 101 course on being an informant. There are some do's and don'ts that have to be abided by you at all times."

"Do I carry a gun from now on?"

"Vic, we don't think that would be in your best interest."

"Yah, but I have this suspicion that they always are carrying in my presence."

"Let's shift gears and get back on track. They are never going to return to Duryea unless we can get the crematory back and running as the bait. It's the key to the whole operation, Vic."

"Well see, there is a financial problem there. The crematory leasing company isn't going to give me another one, if I don't pay them back nearly $50,000 I owe for the one that got destroyed. Before you say insurance, I screwed up there, and don't have any, just for the building."

John knows that the mob is too savvy for a pretend scheme; he needs to build a real crematory in Duryea. They go back and forth the rest of the morning trying to figure out a way to get around this problem.

Finally, Robert says, "Vic, I just got off the phone with my superiors, and here is what we are going to do. You will build a smaller garage for maybe half of the $60,000 insurance and we will come up with the other $20,000 to pay off the retort. This will clear the books with the crematory company and you will be able to lease a new one."

"You might have to up that to $30,000 because they will also want an upfront deposit on the new lease."

"Okay, Vic, consider you have the money and let's get the project rolling."

"If only Sam knew that the FBI was facilitating the new crematory just to help them bring in more bodies," Vic thought to himself.

"We will tap both incoming and outgoing calls on your phones. This will allow us to monitor you when you give Sam updates on the progress of the new crematory. We may even have you invite Sam down for a progress tour at some point. Then we can get pictures and maybe some more critical information."

"Do I really have to meet with him again?"

"Afraid so, Vic, he is your contact with the family. Vinnie appears to be only a low level runner and muscle man."

Vic can attest to the job description for Vinnie.

"You said that you are going to have to go to New York and pick up the next body."

"Yah, that's their way of punishing me for letting the retort burn down."

"We will have you wear a wire for that trip and have your SUV equipped with cameras."

"You don't think these guys are not going to search me and the Suburban?"

"We don't know, but the New York office will be alerted to provide backup should anything get out of hand."

"Out of hand? This sounds like the movies where everyone comes out shooting. Everyone except me who doesn't have a gun, remember?"

"Vic, it is our job to see that it never gets that far. You'll just have to trust us on this."

Sam Tells Almost All

THE SCHEDULED MEETING at Rosselli's is not all wine and roses. During the business session Carlo calls on Sal Travisi to report on his area of collections and enforcement. Sal, looks every bit a seasoned gangster, complete with scars and other markings testifying to an earlier life on the hardened streets of New York. Now a boss, Sal has others to break bones or sometimes wack offenders.

"It is unfortunate that our collections are down, and I feel it is because there is a lack of fear on the street, because nobody is getting whacked for gross infractions of rules and extreme debts. We are owed in excess of $500,000 up from $200,000 a couple of months ago. Worse, we have a couple of "canaries" out on the street who might end up in the clutches of the FBI. These are the most unpredictable of the problems. We just never know when they can be picked up or surrender themselves to the law and start singing. Sal ends his commentary asking when can we start eliminating these problems again?"

For the answer to this, Carlo turns to Sam. "You need to give us the answer, your 'firestop' was the key and now we have lost it."

Sam takes the floor. He is going to tell them most of the facts about the Duryea operation, but keep the details of Victor's negligence out. Sam knows this will only reflect back on him, who at an earlier meeting assured Carlo and the others that he could control Victor even though he was an outsider. So, Sam stays positive. "We have told Victor Kozol that he is to rebuild the crematory post haste. While he has insurance covering the loss, he needs time for permitting and the construction of a new garage. The retort will be the last piece, and then we will be ready to resume "shipments."

"Give us a date," barks Sal. "I don't want to hear how you build a watch, just tell me the time."

Carlo who has heard enough looks at Sam, "You go to Pennsylvania and you get this project expedited ASAP. Further, since this Victor guy has no track record with us, I want him put under surveillance. If he proves to be a traitor, you have my permission to take him out."

"Consider it done," responds Sam.

Meeting adjourned.

Sam now has two reasons for his unannounced trip to Pennsylvania. First, he will stop off and meet with Sonny Boddega, the Don of a smaller and less violent crime family in Northeast Pennsylvania.

With $15,000 in an envelope that he slides towards Sonny while having lunch at the old Train Station Restaurant in Scranton, he makes the deal to watch Victor. He wants Sonny to assign a man to shadow Vic on a full-time basis and also find out about any unusual associates he might be meeting with. He is particularly interested in any law enforcement people hanging around the funeral home in Duryea. He then gives Sonny his cell number so that he can make timely reports. Next, it's off to Duryea.

"Hello, Sam, I didn't expect you today. Please come in."

Once in Vic's office, they go over the details of the project. "Next week the Amish barn builders are coming, and in three days will raise a pole barn over the ruins of the old garage, which has already been cleaned up. If all the permits come through, in another week we can expect the delivery of the new retort. The final thing will be the plumbers and electricians to hook it up. After that a quick final inspection by the Boro and I should be ready to fire it up. I am thinking three weeks at the longest, Sam."

"Okay, but remember we have about $100,000 riding on this and I wouldn't want to be the one to have to answer for a screw up. Right, Vic?"

"Absolutely, Sam."

With Sam gone, Vic is shaking inside, but he hopes that Sam didn't notice how nervous he really was.

Vic now calls John on his private cell. "He was just here, did you get his picture?"

"Who, Vic?"

"You know; Sam."

"You were supposed to call and alert us if he was in town."

"That's the problem. He just walked in on me. I couldn't tell him, excuse me one minute while I alert the FBI, could I?"

"Okay, point taken. Did it go alright?"

"He seemed content when I told him we would be operational in three weeks."

"Good, I'll expedite all your permitting with the Boro and the State so that we actually meet that timetable. Stay lose, Vic, you're doing fine."

John now calls Mike Shoemaker, the fire marshal and says, "Mike I need a favor." He then gives Shoemaker an update of the Kozol investigation I want you to close out the Kozol fire and list it as an accident of undetermined origin. Submit all the paperwork. After this is over, you can file the real report."

"Okay, John, consider it done."

John and the FBI are the silent partners to the mob on this part of the project. What they don't know won't hurt them. The only thing John regrets is that he missed his chance to observe Sam when he was in Duryea. To prevent that from happening again he orders a full-time stakeout on Vic's two properties. He is determined to not let these targets move around unobserved.

As the day is quickly approaching for the installation of the retort, the FBI has to get moving. Vic's suburban is taken to Philadelphia for a day where a crack team of electronics experts install cameras, mics, and a tracking device on the vehicle. The wiring is not the tricky part, it's the concealment that they must be absolutely sure is undetectable.

Meanwhile, Sonny from Scranton has posted a round the clock surveillance guy on Vic. He notices a plain gray Ford seeming to shadow Vic's properties, but doesn't know who it is. It's not the local police, but who? He duly reports to Sonny what he observes. Sonny tells them to keep looking for answers.

Back in New York, Sam receives his first update from Sonny. Yes, Vic is building the new crematory. The ten ton monster piece of equipment has been rolled into the newly completed garage. But, what about the gray, unmarked car shadowing the operation? There seems to be only two answers here; one, the Fire Marshall or some other local police entity is investigating Vic on their own. Two, it could be a unit of the State Police Crime Investigation Department or worse the FBI, which would indicate Vic turned on them.

In either case, Sam doesn't like the new wrinkle and knows he needs insurance that Vic will carry out his end of the operation. If the heat is on too much, Sam will have to terminate the operation—and the operator. This is not a pleasant thought for him, as he will have to once again bear the bad news back to Carlo and the others of another failure.

Pennsylvania is not lost yet, and Sam will only terminate the operation if he has proof of his suspicions. The investigation may be only temporary and it will all blow over; then again it may not. Sam only knows he is not walking away from 'firestop' without trying to salvage it.

"Hello, Sam," Vic says excitedly over the phone. We had our final tests today and the retort is signed off by all local and state inspectors. We are back in business."

"Good work, Vic, you know the drill from here. This time we call you and give you an address in the City, and you come to us for the pick-up."

"Of course, Sam, just give me a little lead time."

Sam hangs up. *And that's just what we won't give him.*

So, how to manage the risks? What if I give him a disaster pouch with no body in it for a trial run? Vic will take it back to Duryea, and if those people who are shadowing him make a move on him there will be no evidence of any crime that could be connected back to the family. Vic would be busted, but even he hasn't broken any laws that they can prove. If Vic is part of the entrapment, we will know if we see him cooperating with authorities back at the crematory. Then we lose our investment and move on; it is a cost of doing business. However, after the smoke clears, Vic will get a visit and come to regret selling us out. "At least," Sam thought, "I finally have a plan."

Tested

VIC AND KAREN are together in her apartment in Scranton. Ever since the start of all this craziness, Karen feels better meeting Vic away from his place. But outside, in an old, beat-up, nondescript van sits an average-looking guy in coveralls with a camera. Sonny has dispatched Mike Gerulo one of his soldiers to shadow Vic trying to get some more intel on him.

Karen and Vic are tense because they know that with the retort being operational the main event is not far off.

Vic says, "I'm glad it's almost over, but like any book, you don't know the ending until you get to the last chapter. For both of us, I hope it's a happy ending."

"Yes, Vic, but what will you do if this all blows over? Go back to slacking off and looking for the next fast buck scheme?"

"Hey, that ain't fair."

"No, but it's true, isn't it?"

"Karen, I want to have a different life. But, I'm just no good at anything. You have nursing; I have a failed funeral home."

"This is our home. We could stay here and build a new life together."

"How? I dig ditches or sell hamburgers?"

"No stupid, you become a *real* funeral director and get your business back. You could even take the crematory as a prize for all of this and make it financially successful."

Chapter 34

"Yah, maybe."

"Look I'll help, we could become a team. You know I am interested in the funeral business; I always told you I want to help you."

"I promise, if I live through this, you and I will work as a team."

"To be a respectable funeral director in a small town, you might have to get married, Vic."

"Are you proposing to me? I accept! It would be wonderful, if we both get that far."

Trial Run

IT'S A FRIDAY evening when Vic gets the call to leave for a warehouse in Brooklyn. He checks in with John who has Gus activate all of the electronics on Vic's Suburban. They are depending on this to track Vic without putting a tail on him. John feels this gang is too street-smart to not discover that ploy. He also has the FBI field office in Brooklyn on standby. They are given the address, but told not to get too close unless they are called by John.

After two-and-a-half hours Vic is outside the warehouse down by the docks. A garage door rolls up, and Vic is motioned in. He is then led out the other end of the building by another black van through a narrow dark alley.

After several turns he, and the escort van, approach a second warehouse and again the door slowly opens and both vehicles drive in. With no lights on two figures dressed in black motion Vic to stop. The back doors of the Suburban are opened a pouch slid in and the doors bang shut. Vic is motioned to back out and told to return to Duryea.

In five minutes it's over. John asks Gus, "What did you get?"

"Not much John, there was not enough light for pictures, the only voice recorded is a muffled command for Vic to return to Duryea."

"Call New York office, see what they got."

"They saw Vic's van go in but it never returned, so they later looked inside and the place was empty. I guess they lost, Vic."

"Tell New York to go home. We won't need them anymore tonight."

John knows that the mob can be very elusive on their own turf.

Just then, the phone rings and it's Vic heading west on Route 80; he is returning with the package; there were no snafus.

John meets Vic at the garage by entering from a back door which is not visible from the street. They pull the pouch from the van and unzip it. It's a dead chimpanzee.

John tells Vic, "We've been set up. They know we are watching and they did this as a safety check. If we swarm the place and you don't call them back, they will know it's over for them and we will never see them again."

Vic is thinking that maybe that's not so bad after all.

John quickly adds, "But that doesn't mean that they won't lie in wait and punish you later."

"So, what do we do?"

"We go on with business as usual, you pretend to do your monkey cremation, dump these ashes I am giving you, and give them their all-clear code.

"I will pull off all surveillance of this place and wait. They will come to one of two conclusions; one that we were setting them up forcing them to respond with a phony shipment. They will suspect the operation is busted and not contact you anymore.

"The other scenario is that they figure whoever was watching you was from a lower level agency like the fire marshal. After not finding anything suspicious they gave up the surveillance. We hope they go with the latter idea and try and ship you a real body in the future. We just have to wait and see."

The Real Deal

TWO WEEKS GO by with no contact. But then on Friday night Vic gets a call from Sam. "Hi, Vic, everything alright in Duryea?"

"Yup, the last guy you sent was kind of small, not like the one before. I guess people come in all shapes and sizes. The crematory works fine and as I informed you the ashes were disposed of." (The chimpanzee was actually sent to a lab in Philadelphia for any forensic evidence it might contain.)

"Okay, Vic, you will be hearing from us."

On the following Monday afternoon, Vinnie calls Vic and tells him he wants him to leave for the same address at the docks in Brooklyn he came to last time. It is now late afternoon when Vic gets the call off to John that he will be on the move to New York. John has Gus fire up all of the surveillance gear in the van. Plus, he alerts the Brooklyn Bureau to be on the lookout. Let the games begin.

"Call us when you are free of the warehouse in Brooklyn heading home, and I will meet you at the garage."

"I'm with you," answers Vic.

Vic is really excited. This could be the end of a long bad dream. He really needs this to happen and be over.

When Vic pulls into the toll booth at the Verrazano narrows bridge, he pays his toll and is handed a note by a shadowy guy standing next to the toll house. Vic pulls off to the side of the road to read the note.

Vic,

We just want you to know that we have Karen. She is safe as long as you complete your mission. Don't call anyone or do anything out of the ordinary or Karen will be in need of your services.

Your friends

Attached to the note is a new address in Brooklyn for Vic to go to. Oh shit, Vic breaks out in a cold sweat. They will kill Karen the same as they did the people in the body bags. It is not thinkable that this is an idle threat; not with these people. I don't dare call John. They may be watching me, and Karen will pay.

With that Vic pulls to the side and rips out the camera buried in the ceiling of his truck and two more in the rear; he then throws away the special cell phone he had and opens the hood and rips out the GPS transmitter. He promptly chucks all of this into a refuse barrel next to him. Then he continues his trip to the new address in Brooklyn.

Back in Wilkes-Barre, panic ensues. Gus hollers, "We don't know what happened. He went through the tolls at the bridge and then everything went dead. We see a hand reaching for the camera, but we don't know, in the dark, who it was. On top of that, Vic is not answering his cell phone. What the hell happened?"

"We can alert the New York Police to look for the SUV, but he could be anywhere after crossing the bridge," says John. Of course, the Brooklyn FBI probably has the wrong warehouse staked out. They will see no activity there. For the moment, John and his team are stymied.

Vic is now at the new address in Brooklyn. This time he is escorted to another pier two blocks away. Vic is led into another abandoned warehouse on a pier. After he stops, Sam steps out of the shadows and Vic confronts him.

"What have you done with Karen? I want to talk to her right now, or I don't take your 'package' with me."

"Sure, Vic," as Sam hands Vic his cell where Vic hears an excited Karen telling him not to worry, they won't hurt her if he does what they ask, this is followed by a dial tone.

"Where is she?"

"Not for you to worry about, Vic, the Pocono Mountains is such a large area."

"Okay, I'll take the package back, but when I send the all clear message I want Karen released unharmed."

"That's the plan. We wouldn't have it any other way. We do, after all want to continue doing business with you. But, after all that recently went down, we needed some insurance that you weren't going to go off the reservation on us."

"Just don't hurt her or I'll . . ."

"You'll what? Listen, Vic, just do your job and everything will be fine."

Petrified, Vic drives back towards Pennsylvania. This time he is being followed by Vinnie in a small black Toyota. He has no idea how this is going to play out, but he knows he has to keep going. The only chance for help is back in Duryea where he is on his, and hopefully Agent John's turf.

The Honeymoon Lodge, five miles from Canadensis, Pennsylvania, is situated in a remote, heavily wooded area. It is here that Karen is to be held in a small cabin at the end of a dirt lane. The resort has ten such cabins, but is closed for the season. They open for business after June first.

Karen has her hands bound in front of her with plastic restraints. The two goons with her, Milt and Johnny, are enforcers from New York. They a waiting for her in the hallway of her apartment after her shift at the hospital.

Karen had enough of a head start to enter her unit and get to her bathroom. But, the locked door was a no barrier for them. It only took a few kicks for the door to be broken down. They grabbed Karen, gagged and bound, unable to scream out or protest. With a gun in her ribs, she went quietly to the car.

As they got close to the lodge Karen realized where she was, since her blindfold had slipped down. She knows, in this isolated spot, screaming will not help. She figures, the only chance is to get loose and try and outrun the two goons.

If only I could get a head start. In this pitch dark I might have a chance.

Meanwhile, Vic is approaching his garage in Duryea. He has no way to warn John and Bob that he is being tailed by Vinnie. Bob is positioned in the shadows outside the garage and John remains inside waiting. Vic, upon pulling up, uses his remote to open the darkened garage and drives in.

Vinnie was given orders to stop about a block from the garage and case the property for any unusual activity. But he is tired, and doesn't see anything unusual, so he drives right up to the garage door behind Vic. The electric door is closing as Vinnie is parking when he suddenly sees a flashlight beam pointed at his face and hears, "FBI freeze."

Vinnie ducks, and gets off a shot in the direction of the light. Almost instantly, three more shots ring out and Vinnie slumps behind the steering wheel gasping his last. Bob runs over from his hiding place and is quickly joined by John.

Victor, standing next to John, looks in and says, "It's Vinnie, my contact. He is the one I always give the all-clear signal after I cremated the body and disposed of the ashes. That's just the half of it John, they have Karen."

"What, how do you know?"

Vic now relates his saga in New York, complete with talking to Karen. Victor excitedly says "The bigger problem is that Vinnie is the one to give the 'release Karen message' to his guys once I completed my mission here. I can't even think what will happen to her when they don't get an all-clear from Vinnie."

Now it's John's turn to be flustered. They search Vinnie and find his cell phone, but it has no numbers stored in the memory. They have no way of reaching out to Karen's abductors by way of Vinnie's phone.

John says, "I just had no idea they would grab my niece for insurance on you going through with your job. Did I ever underestimate the reach of this gang, I am so sorry for my sloppiness here."

John rebounds quickly and asks, "Did you hear them say anything about where they are holding her?"

"Sam just spoke in riddles about the Poconos being an awfully big place."

"He spoke the truth, there are hundreds of square miles between here and the Delaware River."

Karen is now locked away in a cabin with her two abductors. She says "Hey guys, I need to use the bathroom."

"Here Milt, take this beauty queen to the bathroom."

"I'd rather take her to the bedroom."

"Shut up," yells Johnny, "no touching the merchandise on company time idiot!"

"Sure," says Milt, "but if we get the order to whack her, I may just have to use this little honeymoon cabin for my own party first."

That seals the deal for Karen, she needs to escape and fast. After being shoved into the bathroom by Milt, Karen locks the door. There is a window and she tries to nudge it open. At first it doesn't move, then with a scraping noise it opens. Karen opens the faucet and flushes the toilet to make masking noises, while she forces the window toward its fully opened position. With a final crunching noise the old warped window is finally open.

With her hands are still tied, Karen will have to dump herself out of the window head first. She will have no support to help break the fall. If she is caught she will have the bruises from the fall plus a likely beating from the goons to worry about. But, not liking any of her other options decides to go through with the escape.

She lands on her back, fortunately on a soft lawn about five feet down. But the thump and continuous running water have attracted attention. "So much for a big head start," she muses.

Karen hears the banging on the flimsy bathroom door which will soon give way and allow her captors to pursue her. The only chance is to seek cover in the nearby woods. She will have to cover some distance in the thickets and hope to see either a road or house lights in the distance. She needs a target to run towards.

Meanwhile Milt and Johnny having broken down the bathroom door realized Karen is gone.

"Quick out the front door, Johnny yells."

Reaching the side of the cabin where the bathroom is located, they realize it's pitch dark and they forgot their flashlight. Another minute is lost, allowing Karen to get out of earshot of the cabin. But, progress is slow as the brambles and thick underbrush are scratching her legs causing bleeding. Karen is running on adrenaline and doesn't even notice.

John raced up to the Scranton Hill Section where Karen's apartment is located. The local police are already there and have started to search the empty apartment. John figures, since the door frame is splintered, Karen was hold up here and overheard them mention the name which she wrote with lipstick "Honeymoon Lodge" on the inside of the closet door. Good thinking, because if she used the mirror or someplace more prominent they would have seen the message and erased it.

John made a quick call to the State Police for the location of "Honeymoon Lodge" in the Poconos. It turns out there are two. One is far over in Hazleton off Route 80 and the other is in Canadensis, closer to Scranton. John barks, "Tell the Hazleton barracks to check out their lodge, and have the Mount Pocono barracks checkout the Canadensis one. I'd put my money on Canadensis. It's closer. Have a chopper pick me up on the roof of the CMC hospital."

Meanwhile, the chase is on for Karen. Fortunately, Milt and Johnny are big city boys, not deer hunters. They could much easier catch you in a five story tenement in New York than here. But, Karen isn't home free. With her hands still bound Karen can make only slow progress, and the terrain has turned marshy. The escape and search went on for twenty minutes. Tiring, Karen leans on a branch; it cracks, dumping her onto the ground.

"What was that noise, Milt?"

"I don't know, but it came from over by that swamp."

The two goons head towards the swamp. Just when Karen was trying to be quiet, a raccoon scampers in front of her and she screams.

"Now we got her!"

The two hurry over towards Karen finding her on the ground.

"You caused us a lot of trouble little lady, now we are going to cause some for you," seethes Johnny.

They roughly yank Karen out of her hiding place and march her back towards the cabin. Back at the cabin everyone is panting from the walk when Johnny sees a message on his cell.

It's Sam, "Vinnie didn't give us a signal and we can't raise him on his cell. Whack the girl and get back to the City and lay low."

"You heard the orders Milt, let's do it."

They had one chance to get away clean, but the thugs didn't know it. Time was not on their side. They should have executed Karen and cleared out ASAP. But Milt wants his party with Karen first. Johnny, sensing danger, wants to split, but Milt says just ten minutes. He takes the bloodied Karen into the bedroom cutting loose her hands. She protests and bucks, but he again rams his gun into her ribs. He then ties her hands and feet to the bedposts. Karen spits in Milt's face. He just smiles and wipes it off. Milt begins ripping her clothes off and then removes his own. This is the moment he has been waiting for since he first laid eyes on her.

"Freeze FBI!" Johnny, knowing they have the drop on him surrenders. But, Milt goes for his pistol and comes out shooting. He goes down with one shot to the head. Standing on the porch with his service pistol out is FBI Agent John Flaherty, who just landed ten minutes earlier and then jumped into a State Police car for the short drive to the resort.

He persuaded the state police to let him go in first and try to save his niece. Had Karen not escaped, and Milt not let his hormones run wild, Karen could have been executed and the killers been safely on their way back to New York. That was way too close.

Celebration

AT A FAMILY party at Karen's parents' house, there was much to celebrate. Uncle John had secured immunity for Victor in return for his testimony against the Dellveccio Family. The surviving kidnapper of Karen, Johnny, was cooperating with the FBI. He named several names of family operators, but most importantly, named Sam Gianetti, the lawyer as his boss. In addition, Sam was named by Victor as his contact that financed and controlled the illegal crematory. This was a coup, as Gianetti was the highest member of the Dellveccio family to be indicted in anyone's memory. To get "capos" indicted at all was a rare occurrence for law enforcement. Even more importantly, the illegal cremation operation was closed early. Letters went out to all crematory owners and manufactures to be suspicious and report any attempts of being approached concerning illegal activities.

Sitting in the corner of the dining room is Aunt Sophie. She is the one person not smiling and celebrating at the family party. Sophie is not so sure that everything is over with the mob. She knew a friend from Queens, New York, who once told her that the mob does not forgive or forget. They have a long memory and punish people who are either traitors or failures in their ventures. Wasn't this what their recent cremation scheme with Victor was all about anyway? It was vengeance for people who screwed up. Sophie knew that if they could grab and nearly kill her niece once, they were capable of finishing the job. She needed a plan, but didn't even think of telling her fears to Agent John; he would just think her just another crazed old crank. No, Sophie needed proof, but how to find it?

Agent John also learned a lesson—to not underestimate the mob as they got way too close to his niece for comfort. However, he didn't feel that there would be anymore reaction from the mob in Pennsylvania, because the Dellveccio's didn't need any more legal trouble. He would be proven right on that scenario, but wrong on the theory of "Murphy's Law"; if something can go wrong it probably will. Anyway the party ended on a high note and all were happy that a good future awaited the soon to be wed couple.

The Unraveling

BACK IN NEW York, things were not going well for Sam. Both he and Sal are under indictment by the Feds. Sal has already been reprimanded and demoted for his sloppy supervision of the two soldiers that kidnapped Karen. Carlo, the family Don, was not about to take this embarrassment lightly. However for Sam, the golden boy who had the brains and education to lead the family into a new generation, his dream was crushed. Sam was now an anathema to Carlo.

In retrospect, Carlo thought it crazy to trust this cremation scheme to an operator who was an outsider and over a hundred miles from the City. The function of destroying bodies that they had eliminated was too serious of an endeavor to handle it the way Sam did. Carlo now had to find lawyers to defend his people, and possibly replace them when they went to prison. It was particularly galling to have to hire a lawyer to defend your lawyer. Carlo so much wished he were back in the much simpler and better 'olden days'.

Sam is livid and depressed at the same time. He goes from first in line to head the family to an indicted felon. Worse, there is this kid Victor, who is about to skate out of all of this as if it never happened and he had nothing to do with it.

Sam can't get his mind around these facts. He is at home drinking and getting angrier by the minute. Worst debacle the family had in ten years, and he is the fall guy for it. Oh, it was fine when the bodies were disappearing and everyone was 'fat, dumb, and happy'. But to think that little weasel in Pennsylvania is riding high, and I may be going to prison. . . . The more Sam thought about it, the more he started screaming, "Retribution is mine and mine alone!" He was going to get even, and he was going to do it personally.

Sam knew that Carlo had written off "operation firestop", and would take his losses. He further knew Carlo would not risk any more assets trying to get even with Victor. Sam alone was going back to Duryea.

Duryea

IT IS FRIDAY evening, Vic and Karen are together in the funeral home apartment. They have been repainting and decorating the downstairs to be more inviting to the clientele. Upstairs they are making a nest for themselves, as Victor finally has something to live for. No more, excess drinking, gambling, or lying around feeling lethargic. This was a new day and thanks to Karen and her Uncle John, Vic would be around to celebrate it.

The fall night was cold and blustery, and the couple turned in early. Vic thought he heard a noise downstairs. He listened, but not hearing anything else he rolled over and went back to sleep. Suddenly, he and Karen are staring down the barrel of Sam's Glock pistol. Sam was standing at the foot of the bed in his black trench coat with a look of cold rage.

"You two lovebirds have ruined my life and now you are going to pay."

Vic stammers, "Wait a minute, I was trapped."

"Sure you were and this little niece of Agent John. Well, we are going to have a going away party tonight, just the three of us. Get your coats on. We are going for a little ride."

"Where?"

"You know; the crematory."

Vic drove his Suburban, Karen rode shotgun, and Sam sat in the back.

"Drive straight to the garage, or you two will be missing what little brains you have."

Vic and Karen are the most frightened they have ever been. The atmosphere was a lot more toxic than any other threats or the kidnapping of Karen. Vic's adrenaline is pumping, but he knows that to get shot in the back by being brave won't help.

Sam screams, "Open the garage door and drive in."

Vic, thinking fast, wants to say he doesn't have the opener, but it is hanging on the sun visor right above him, so he complies and drives in. The lights from the headlights of Vic's SUV cast an eerie glow inside.

Pointing the gun at Vic Sam bellows, "Get out and walk over in front of the retort!"

Vic does what he is told.

"Now open the door!"

Vic pushed the open button and the hydraulically powered door slid up, revealing the cavernous space of the fire chamber.

"Get in!" Sam orders.

"You can't."

"Shut up, I said crawl in or I execute you here on the spot. That would give me almost as much pleasure as standing here with your girlfriend as I start the retort and listen to you die inside."

Karen notices that all of Sam's attention is now on Vic, and the garage door is open. She bolts for the opening and gets almost to freedom when a bullet bites into her left shoulder. Karen is stunned, but hoping it's a flesh wound keeps running. She continues to run. Sam's second shot goes wild because Vic gives him a shove just as he fires at Karen again.

If Sam were thinking right he would finish off Victor and then catch up to, and finish off, the wounded Karen. But Sam is too enraged and can't get the scenario out of his mind of cremating Vic alive. He backhands Vic with his pistol. Vic falls in front of the retort and pretends to be knocked out cold. Thinking Vic is taken care of, for now, Sam leaves him behind and rushes outside to pursue Karen.

Karen, not knowing where to run, stays on the street heading away from the garage. Sam spots her white coat reflecting off a streetlight at the next intersection. He darts through a wooded area hoping to head her off before she can make it so the next intersection and the safety of some houses. It is just before the second intersection that Sam surprises Karen, who confused, hesitates as she looks for which way to turn. She is also getting light-headed from loss of blood.

"Alright girl, we are now going back. This time I finish you off right here if you make one sound. Now march!"

Upon entering the garage with Karen ahead of him, Sam scans the retort, but there is no Vic lying there. He turns around with his gun still drawn looking for Vic. But, still no Vic anywhere in sight, just shadows and silence. Sam walks towards the retort where he last saw Vic, when out of the corner of his eye sees Vic coming at him with a leftover piece of two by four.

Sam holds up his right arm to deflect the blow; however this is his shooting arm and his gun is knocked loose and slides under the Suburban.

Sam says, "I hadn't planned on killing you with my bare hands, but it will give me great pleasure."

Vic is now too pumped up to stop, so he lands a second blow on Sam's shoulder. Sam grabs the plank and rips it from Vic's hand. Vic immediately closes the distance with Sam and begins to wildly pummel him with his fists.

Out of nowhere Aunt Sophie appears with a pavement brick and smashes it into Sam's face just as he is about to land a round-house on Vic.

Sam's legs buckle from Sophie's blow and his upper body slumps into the opening of the retort. Vic is trying to hold Sam's lower body against the retort so that he can't get any leverage. Karen, unfortunately weak from her gunshot, is slumped on the floor and can be of no help.

Vic yells, "Sophie, push the second red button!" Sophie searches for the button, but Sam is beginning to slip out of Vic's grip; just then the hydraulic door began to close, clamping Sam's head between the closing door and the floor of the retort. Sam screams, but the pressure crushes his skull as Sophie refuses to release her pressure on the button. In two more seconds Sam goes quiet—his life is over.

Vic and Karen are once again surrounded by police and EMT personnel. Karen is taken to the hospital with Vic left to answer questions to the authorities. Sam's body, released from the retort, lies dead on the floor. Sophie stands silently in the background.

Later at CMC hospital, Vic is in Karen's room and she is sitting up looking much better than at the garage. Her wounds are superficial, but they did cause a considerable loss of blood. Sophie is seated in the one chair looking on.

"Sophie, how did you get there?"

"Well, every Friday, I have dinner with Esther at the Silver Bell Dinner in Duryea. I never was satisfied that this thing was over, so after finishing, I got in my car and instead of going right home I decided to cruise by your funeral home. Parked at a funny angle was this large gray Lincoln with New York plates. I thought this was suspicious, so I parked and walked up to your place and rang the bell. When I didn't get an answer, I walked around the back and saw the door wide open, but nobody there. I didn't know where to look, but I knew of your crematory down the street, so I just decided to go there.

When I saw your SUV lights on and heard voices, I crept up to the door, and, well, you know the rest."

"Sophie, I can't tell you how much that intuition meant to Karen and me, but any hard feelings I had towards you are gone. And, you have my sincere apologies for the past."

Duryea Revisited

IT HAS BEEN some time since the violence culminating in the drama ending with Sam's death at the crematory. The tally is: Victor up one, and the syndicate lawyer Sam, Milt, and Vinnie all dead; plus, another mob soldier and his boss indicted by the feds. However, there are other closer to home consequences to all of this. To have a shootout between the FBI and the mob in Duryea is not everyday news. And how many mob lawyers get their heads crushed in a crematory retort? This is more like having Martians landing in the town. People can't stop talking, and the local papers have run countless features on their front pages.

Finally, the local TV stations were interviewing anyone willing to comment on the events, and running the clips on the local evening news. The once bumbling Vic is now a huge celebrity. But, is he a good guy or a villain? If John Flaherty and the FBI are willing to spin it that Vic was helping in an undercover operation from the beginning that would be one thing. However, if it comes out that Vic initiated all of these events because of his underworld dealings public opinion might be much different. Will the Justice Department allow a report that shows Victor in a good light?

Vic's lawyer, Steve Lamont, is in a case more complex and higher up the legal food chain, than any other local lawyer has ever seen. The authorities and Steve work out a compromise in which Vic admits to some initial wrongdoing. But, then they must concede the fact that he risked his and Karen's life to help apprehend the criminals. He is now a genuine local hero.

Most people in Duryea want to believe the second part of Vic's role because in a small town, even an unpopular local trumps a crime family from New York. Vic will get a pass on the initial illegal cremations since he didn't participate in or was he complicit in the actual murders of those individuals. In exchange, he has to agree to testify as a government witness as to his part in any trial of those mob family members now under indictment.

A Future

VIC AND KAREN both know they have to make something positive happen with their lives. Karen has always been ambitious, but Vic needed a whole new makeover after his life had been turned upside down.

"Vic, you have to put the same effort into your future as you used to put in college beer parties."

She then gives him an ultimatum. "Vic, I am not getting any younger. I am now twenty-eight, and you are what I have to show for my social life up to this point.

We either make this work together, or I am out of here. I can't say being with you hasn't been, to say the least, exciting. And, no one can hold a candle to the experiences you and I have gone through. But, this is not how two people who love each other should spend their lives together. We seem to just be going from crisis to crisis."

"I need time to sort all of this out, Karen, maybe we could just continue to see each other until all of this is behind us."

"No, Vic, that is not how this is going to go down. If I walk out this door tonight, I am gone for good. I want no more procrastinating, lethargic spells lasting for weeks, or indecision about your future. I will not stay with a man who continues the behavior you have in the past. So, what's it going to be?"

"Karen, I love you, but I have to be sure that I can provide a future for the two of us."

"I love you too, but I will not hesitate to come down on you worse than the mob if you ever revert to your former ways."

"I understand, Karen, I needed that."

With that Vic gets down on one knee and says, "I am tired of whining and thinking of what might have been, I promise to be a man you will be proud of. Will you marry me?

"Yes, yes, we can rebuild our lives right here where we have family and friends to support us."

"I think I know how to rebuild the business I trashed. It could make for a good living for us as it had for my family for three generations. Then, we can tell our parents and start planning for a new life together."

Karen's parents, Fred & Sue Schmidt, are more urbane and liberal than Vic's people. Since neither of them came from a small town, they see things with a more cosmopolitan view. They now live in Scranton, a city of seventy-five thousand, which is ten times the size of Duryea. Fred, a transplant from Philadelphia, is a foreman at a local plastics plant and Sue is a pharmacist's assistant at a local drug store. They are actually thrilled that their oldest of two daughters is going to marry Vic. They believe him to be intelligent and personable, and hope that he will do what is necessary to make the marriage successful. Their youngest daughter Jean is already married with a baby.

Vic's side of the family is a bit more complicated. The provincial leanings of his parents show through when they come to Duryea to meet the future Mrs. Kozol.

Albert says, "Vic she might be a nice girl, but her name is Karen Schmidt, and with a mother's name like Flaherty, we don't see one ounce of Polish heritage here."

Vic's mother chimes in, "A German father and an Irish mother might be fine in Scranton, but what will people say here in Duryea?"

"Look Mom, she is after all, Catholic and educated, with a profession. Her new last name will be Kozol not Schmidt. I think she will do fine, even if she doesn't speak Polish. By the way neither do I!

She will be a great partner to help me salvage this business. Karen is a people person who makes friends and fits in. Look Dad, I want you to reconsider about the business, if you sell it now, you will get little more than the property value."

"All the years I trusted you, Vic, and you always fell short of your promises and my expectations. I am going to reserve final judgment on the business until later. As for you and Karen, you have our blessings to get married. That is, if she agrees to get married at Holy Rosary Church with Father Sosnowski officiating."

"Always thinking of the business dad, we'll see."

Karen and Vic were married in an old fashioned Polish style ceremony that spring. First, there was the concelebrated Mass with three Priests (one a cousin of the family from Cleveland) and of course two vocalists one who sang "Ave Maria." A parade of four white limousines carried the bridal party around town that warm and sunny May day.

Next, was the reception at the church social hall with three-hundred in attendance. There was kielbasa, pierogi, kuegele, ham, and turkey. In addition a seven tier wedding cake with the ubiquitous miniature bridal couple on the top graced the head table. There was also enough beer, wine, liquor, and other beverages to last for two days, a five piece polka band, Franky and the Coal Miners, to keep the tempo upbeat. There was a bridal dance where everyone lines up to put money in a hat for a dance with the bride. With three-hundred attendees each dance lasts about 10 seconds. This is followed by the 'kidnapping' of the bride by the attendants. After a suitable time, Vic rescues Karen by paying a ransom to the best man; Karen is then returned to her groom.

The next day the couple flies to Bermuda for a non-Polish honeymoon.

Clouds on the Horizon

UPON RETURNING FROM Bermuda, Karen and Vic settle into the apartment above the funeral home in Duryea. They get busy scrubbing, cleaning and polishing the funeral home. Vic is now getting at least a funeral a week—which for him is the best it's ever been. After a month has gone by, they have not heard from Albert. So, Vic calls Florida.

"Dad, we should sit down and talk about my future. You said after the wedding, we could sit down and talk about me buying out the business."

"Vic, what I said was that we would talk about it afterward."

"Well, this is the time."

"Okay, then here is the problem. Mom and I went through some horrendous months last year. There were the late payments from you, the fire, the bad reports from the townspeople about your actions. I saw the books. Half of the business is gone. What took two generations to build you destroyed in a couple of years. We don't think we can risk our retirement on the premise that you can turn around an already damaged business."

"Are you telling me that after all of the promises I made to Karen, plus getting myself psyched up to finally do something here, that it's over?"

"Well you see Vic, my old friend John Postupack in Wilkes-Barre, has a son Bob who got his Funeral license a couple of years ago. He has been working at the Driscoll funeral home down there, and would like to have his own place. So, John and I sort of have a handshake deal where he would take Duryea off my hands. Look, Vic, you always said you didn't want the business. It was I who was forcing you to do something you never wanted to do in the first place. What you did in your first year was just short of criminal negligence."

"Okay, you have made up your mind, but don't expect me to hang around and show the new guy the ropes. We are out of here now."

"Let's not be too hasty here, I'll pay you to help make a smooth transition to the new owner."

"Dad, I don't want your money, I would rather sell apples on Public Square in Wilkes-Barre than kowtow under this ultimatum. Karen and I will move to her place next week, and you can get one of your old cronies to cover the place until you do the deal with Postupack. I have never been so hurt and humiliated! You can have your wedding present back too!"

With that Vic slams down the phone and is seething and kicking things around the apartment.

Karen arrives later that night after her shift at the hospital and surveys the mess. This time Vic is not drinking, he is just sitting in his corner chair staring into space. Vic tells Karen the entire sad episode with his father. She is devastated too, as she told her entire family about her new life centered around the funeral home, now down the drain with one phone call.

"Do you think your father would reconsider, Vic?"

"Hell no, he already has the joint sold. Once he takes action, right or wrong, he carries it through."

"Well, I guess I have to call my landlord in Scranton and ask him to stay. I think he will say alright. But now we need a new future. I can keep my job at the hospital, but you Vic will have to decide what you will do for the future. I am just so sorry for you, Vic."

Vic contacts a couple of old friends, who agree to help him move some of his furniture to Scranton. However, most of his things won't fit since Karen has an already furnished one bedroom apartment. His friend Mike Elchock has a large garage and offered to let Vic keep some of his furnishings there. After a couple of days, reality has set in deeper about the loss of the funeral home.

Karen remarks, "What are you going to do about the cremation retort? We still own that."

"First, I only have a lease on it, secondly it sits in my father's garage."

"Vic, what if we buy or rent the garage from your father, and keep the cremation business as a separate entity? Could it work as a separate business?"

"Well maybe, but I would need to do a couple hundred cases a year for it to make financial sense. Plus, we have no money to buy the garage from my father."

"Let me talk to my father," Karen interjects. If he would loan us the down payment, we could buy the garage from Albert. We would at least have an income."

"Dad, it's Vic. Look, I'm sorry I blew up at you last week. The whole thing was too much for me to grasp at one time. However, I have had time to cool down and think and would now like to cut a deal with you."

"Apology accepted, what can I do for you son?"

"As you know the crematory lease is in my name, but you own the new garage I had rebuilt with the insurance proceeds. I would like to lease the garage with an option to buy it from you. I could then continue to run the cremation business independent of the funeral home."

"Geez, Vic, the new buyer already asked to include the garage in the sale of the funeral home. He is buying new cars and needs room to store them."

"Okay then, I will have to get the retort out of there. Can you give me some time?"

"Yes, Vic, but in exchange you can help me by staying in Duryea until the new owner can close the sale."

Vic is once again nowhere and now has to either give the crematory retort back to the manufacturer or find a new home for it. He and Karen are sitting together in the funeral home apartment and realize that all is slipping away.

Karen says, "Vic, your friend Mike who is letting you store your excess furniture has that big old garage five blocks from here. Maybe we could lease it and move the retort into it?'

Vic calls Mike who agrees to a three year lease on the property subject to Vic getting all of the zoning and other approvals for a crematory.

Vic now has a plan, but no money. Just moving the retort will cost $5,000 not to mention hookups and remodeling. Karen comes through again.

"Vic, I talked to my parents and they will loan us $20,000 to move, remodel, and have working capital to start-up the crematory business. They want no interest, but you can pay it back in the first three years of operations."

"Karen I can't take charity, what if I fail again?"

"First, it's a loan. Not charity. Second, Vic, you won't fail. Together we will make this work. Let's take the offer."

CHAPTER 43

Starting Over

VIC FINALLY HAS a way forward, giving him new energy and resolve. First, he shows Bob Postupack around and orients him to the funeral home he is buying from Vic's dad. Here, Vic notices that this guy has no personality and the people skills of a robot. While not surly, Bob is clipped and almost military-like in his responses. Vic tells him that all the embalming chemicals are in the closet next to the morgue. Bob's response was, "Roger that, copy." This is just something to file away for future reference as Bob will be dealing with the Kozol families. Vic has his own future to deal with.

Karen and Vic are living in her apartment in Scranton, eight miles from Duryea. Vic is commuting back and forth setting up his new business. He gets all the approvals and has the 10 ton retort relocated one mile away to Mike's garage. Carpenters build a small office up front and electricians are busy hooking up the retort. Next, Vic forms a Pennsylvania Corporation. The Duryea Crematory, LLC is now ready to commence operations.

Since Vic is not in the funeral business, it is now much easier promote it to the area funeral directors. But, the big news is that the nearby and closest crematory, Evergreen Cemetery, is going to discontinue cremations because the owners are old and want to retire. Their obsolete equipment needs expensive fire brick relining. Also, it won't pass the EPA's more stringent pollution requirements.

Here are two hundred cases only five miles away. If Vic can capture most of this business he will be a success from day one. He can charge the directors, $300 per case and do it for about $100 including costs. He could then clear $40,000 a year. He never made that much in his failing little funeral home. Vic and Karen have a reception for the area funeral directors. (Vic knows how to provide beer, wine, and snacks to party attendees.)

That evening, they welcome nearly fifty guests with their wives. Karen and Vic meet and schmooze the people like pros. Most are interested in the new service and the ones that are only there to be on the 'find out committee' won't matter anyway. Vic, with Karen's and her family's help, is on his way to his first successful venture in his life.

Success

IF YOU DON'T count the time that Vic was earning thousands for mob cremations, this was the first time in his life that he is finally successful financially. He is easily making the rent and lease payments on his crematory. Because the funeral directors pay Vic up-front for each case as he does them, he has a ready and steady cash flow. He now can finally focus on his and Karen's personal needs. They want to get out of Karen's small apartment in Scranton and find a more suitable home for a family to live in. They are looking around Duryea at some larger apartments and even some homes that they might be able to afford.

Karen again seems to be in the right place at the right time. Duryea has an old time drugstore/pharmacy in the downtown district. Dating back to the early nineteen hundreds it is a well-known area landmark. It has large windows with awnings that roll out on the outside, and inside there is a marble soda fountain with the old stainless steel dispensing equipment still in use. There even is a wooden barrel standing on the counter that dispenses draft birch beer. They make Cokes by putting syrup in a glass and then adding carbonated water. The large globe incandescent lights hang from a metal embossed ceiling. This place is right out of central casting for an old movie. Karen is there to pick up some allergy medications. So, she goes to the back of the store where the pharmacy window is and gets in line. She is standing behind two older women waiting for their turn with the pharmacist.

After eavesdropping, inadvertently, on the conversation her ears perk up when she hears that the speaker is a Mrs. Borovich. She is relating a story to her friend about her husband Jake Borovich. Jake is a longtime Polish Funeral Director in Duryea, and a competitor to Vic's old family funeral home. It seems that Jake had a severe paralyzing stroke earlier in the year. Unable to conduct funerals, it was the family's duty to notify the State Board of Funeral Directors.

To continue, they would have to hire a licensed Funeral Director to serve as supervisor to operate Jake's business. After a couple of attempts, Maria Borovich, can't find anybody interested in being a supervisor. However, Jake did have a handyman that he trained to embalm bodies, direct funerals, and do much of the other technical and professional work when Jake was away or indisposed. All of this is illegal under State law, but as in many small funeral operations, no one is going to complain unless something goes wrong. Jake's wife was lulled into complacency because old Ned the handyman was carrying on with the funerals quite well. He was even forging Jake's signature on the death certificates.

Being a small town, the third funeral director a Joe Jaresky knows exactly what is going on. Joe files a written complaint with the State Board of Funeral Directors in Harrisburg spelling out these violations. After sending in an investigator, the State Board has a hearing two weeks later they notify Mrs. Borovich to cease and desist from operating the funeral home unless she can find a supervisor immediately. She is also fined for the violations.

After three weeks, she is unable to hire anyone and notifies the State Board. This results in an immediate order to close the funeral home, de-list the phone number, and take in the outside sign. In one fell swoop the Borovich Funeral Home, after forty years of operations, is out of business.

Joe Jaresky hopes to capitalize on this and get some of Borovich's business. However, Borovich's friends were outraged upon learning that Jaresky caused all of this just when the Borovich's were up against it.

Karen can't help but take all of this in with increased interest. She sees a possible opportunity for her and Vic in all of this. Karen rushes home and relates all of this to Vic.

Vic says, "Yeh, I feel sorry for Jake, but not Joe Jaresky. He was an opportunist in all of this."

Karen comes back with, "Vic, what if we offer to buy the place from Maria Borovich and reactivate it using your license and name?"

"Well, the Borovich name is over, but I could call it the Victor Kozol Funeral Home."

Karen responds, "And what is wrong with your name in this town after all of the heroic publicity you got? Plus we need a place to live. This could double as our new home."

"Okay Karen, issue settled, I will make an overture to Mrs. Borovich."

Vic made an appointment to see Mrs. Borovich at the funeral home. Things have not improved for the Borovichs. Jake had to be placed in a nursing home and Maria lives in a place far too big for her alone. They agree that after getting the property appraised, Vic could buy the property and the funeral home equipment would go along with the deal.

Vic observes that the place is old and needs remodeling; however it is bigger and better laid out with more land around the house than his old funeral home. There is a three car garage in the back lot and enough room to put in a twenty car parking lot right behind the funeral home. These were both things that the old Kozol Funeral Home lacked.

Vic is now on his way to a second deal in one year with no help from his parents. He secures a $150,000 loan from a local bank on the strength of his cash flow from his now very profitable crematory. He knows a couple of in-town funeral directors might not use his crematory when he goes into the funeral business, but the out-of-town directors won't care. The trade-off should be more than worth it.

After studying Jake's books he sees that the place was doing about thirty-five funeral per year. Not great, but a base to expand from. The apartment is out of the 1950s, but it is large with three bedrooms. Karen thinks it is great, because it is twice the size of the old funeral home apartment above his father's place. For the second time a very positive thing is happening for Vic and Karen.

Epilogue

VIC AND KAREN have never been busier. Karen has quit her nursing job in Scranton and is now the number one assistant to Vic around the funeral home. She is also the secretary for the business. Vic is finally that PR person his father always wanted him to be. He is involved in the community and his church. You can actually see him and Karen attending the 10:00 a.m. Mass every Sunday at Holy Rosary. Fred Schmidt, Karen's father, has taken an early retirement from the plastics plant and is running the crematory for Vic. His mechanical skills fit in perfectly to operate and maintain a sophisticated piece of equipment like a retort.

Vic is so busy with funerals that he needed help on all fronts. He has hired an intern from the Northampton Funeral Service School to serve his one-year residency at the funeral home. This doesn't count the three part timer retirees who drive and help with the business. For the first time, Vic is fully involved with the funeral business. His client families are being given the service and attention they deserve, and they are responding positively to Vic's new funeral business.

Word on the street is try Vic, he is doing a great job and is a caring and compassionate operator. Not to mention that the bodies now look like they should at viewings and the place is clean and neat. The funeral volume, just the first year, climbed to sixty-five and the crematory did over 250 cases in addition. Where did this nearly doubling of the business come from? Well

Vic calls his place Victor Kozol Funeral Home successor to Jake Borovich.

He not only kept all of Jake's old clients, but took a big chunk of work from Joe Jaresky since Jake's widow recommended Vic everywhere she went telling her story of Joe's disloyalty in taking down her husband. The third piece of business came from his old place now run by Bob Postupack. Bob seems to not be able to relate to his client families with his robotic, clinical personality. Vic, with the family name, is right there to take in the disgruntled client families.

Karen is now pregnant with her first child due in five months. Vic feels that he can grow to over one hundred funerals in the near future as Joe Jaresky has put his place up for sale and poor Bob Postupack has filed for bankruptcy. He feels sorry that his father was caught holding a second mortgage on the place and stands to lose $50,000.

However, Vic is letting no moss grow under his feet. He has bought a lot on the outskirts of Duryea and is planning on building a new funeral home with no steps for the elderly and an adequately sized chapel that will seat up to one hundred fifty people. There will be parking for over fifty cars and it will be the only one designed to be a funeral home in the area. In three years, Vic has gone from the bad boy in the town to a success story no one would have predicted. The unsung hero in all of this is Karen who made Vic the person he is now. Even Aunt Sophie tends the front door for Vic at Lithuanian viewings.

Author's Note

I HAVE TRIED to create this novel in a real-world context. I have no proclivities for science fiction or supernatural writing, so you won't find it here. The Anthracite Coal Region of Northeast Pennsylvania is filled with a mosaic of rich landscape, culture, and traditions. These descendants of Eastern European immigrants are no less a part of Americana than anyone else written about. They are warm and charming people who have remained true to their birthplace and celebrate it through their unique culture. There is not much in fiction devoted to this area and its people. If you hear about an ethnic area in Pennsylvania it will usually be about the Amish. I thought I would introduce readers to something different.

Yes, these characters are real and could be anywhere in America. However, this is the America I know best.

I hope you enjoyed following Victor Kozol in his journey.

About the Author

BORN AND RAISED in Allentown, Pennsylvania. The Weber family had operated a funeral home there since 1928. Jerry first graduated Temple University in Philadelphia and then graduated from the American Academy of Funeral Service in New York City. He later received a BA in History from Wilkes University in Wilkes-Barre, Pa. After serving in the US Army in Vietnam, he joined his father and uncle in the family business. After his father's retirement he became the owner of the business. This included three funeral homes and a cemetery.

Jerry has been married for 46 years to Cynthia Wisniewski who was a nursing educator and also a Pennsylvania licensed funeral director. They have two married daughters. Annette lives in Baltimore, MD and Natalie in Berlin, Germany. They have five grandchildren. Jerry flew airplanes and is a commercial pilot. He is also interested in Antique Automobiles and is a judge for the Antique Automobile Club of America. Jerry and Cynthia reside in Venice, Florida.

Preview: Thunder in the Coal Mine

Book II Victor Kozol series

AT NOON ON a Wednesday in May, Karen takes a call from New York City. It is the Harlem Funeral Home with a "trade call". These are calls to funeral homes from other funeral homes usually out of town asking the local funeral director to pick up and prepare a body that is to be transported back to the originating funeral home. Mr Doaks, the New York Director tells Karen that a Josepf Younnes, now deceased, has been released by the coroner from the CMC Hospital in Scranton. He would like the Kozol firm to do the local removal and prep work and get the death certificate and removal permit so that Younnes's body could be transported back to New York. He tells Karen, after all of the arrangements are completed by Kozol's he will make arrangements to pick up the body. Karen takes all of this information and then pages Vic who is out on another funeral.

Vic returns to Duryea and gets on this new mission. First, he calls the Lackawanna coroner's office to see if the body has in fact been released. After getting an affirmative answer, He dispatches his intern and one of the handymen to go to Scranton with the van and get Younnes body.

Later after embalming and preparing the body he comes out of his morgue and begins to think, this guy really is a mess not even viewable for a funeral service. What happened? Vic rounds up the Scranton Times from the last two days and starts looking for accidents to square with the condition of the body. Sure enough, on Monday night there was an explosion at the Northeast Stone Quarry in Peckville about ten miles from Scranton. It seems Younnes who was an equipment maintenance man on the night shift at the quarry was handling some of the dynamite the quarry uses in its daily operations to blast loose the solid rock formations.

Vic is confused by this. Why is a guy who is greasing and maintaining the trucks and other equipment handling explosives? Did he have to move some of the dynamite to get access to something? Was he called by his foreman to change his routine and work with the dynamite? Vic's thoughts are interrupted by another death call that he had to attend to.

The next day a van arrives from New York with a driver to pick up Younnes for his trip back to New York. Vic, while helping the driver load the body, begins thinking about the strange death circumstances, again becoming curious. He is talking a John Merrill who is the man sent to retrieve the body. After presenting John with the death certificate and transit permit the New York firm will need to complete the funeral, Vic strikes up a conversation with him.

"John, what kind of a clientele do you handle up there in the Bronx?"

"Well we do a mix of everyone up there. This Younnes guy is a member of a group that seems to be clustered around a Mosque on 125th Street. They are a pretty conservative group and stay to themselves. One interesting thing is that in the City we are all unionized. The gravediggers at the cemetery have their own union and you have to use them for any burial in one of our cemeteries. But, the members of this group insist on taking shovels and burying their deceased themselves. The union allows this because they stand there and get paid anyway. It's amazing the vastly different customs that are practiced, especially in a big city like New York. Vic asks, "John, do you ever talk to any of them at the funerals?"

"Naw, they are respectful but very cool and aloof around strangers."

With that Vic bids John goodbye and safe journey and goes back to setting up for the Oravitz funeral, which is scheduled to take place tomorrow.

CPSIA information can be obtained
at www.ICGtesting.com
Printed in the USA
FSOW02n0533180217
30810FS